DADDY'S HOME

Robbed of her innonence, betrayed
by family, she must turn to the only life
she knows.

JMPublishings

ISBN: 978-0-692-44286-9

Editor: 21st Street Urban Editing (Niccole Simmons)
www.21streeturbanediting.com

Cover Designs: Donna Osborn Clark at
www.CreationsByDonna.com

Interior Design and Typesetting by
www.interiorbookdesigns.com

Janae Marie Contact info:
Email address: jmpublishings@gmail.com
Website address: www.youngurbanvoices.com
www.krysrieon.wix.com/jmpublications

I dedicate this book to my beautiful baby girl, Kayla. I hope when you grow up you look back and am proud of me. Love you!

Chapter 1

Her Silent Cries

E very night I had to hide. Every night I had to hide from the pain I felt inside. I had to escape from the world I was in. The days he, my father, would come home drunk, yelling and screaming as my mother would leave me alone with him as she rushed off to work as a district attorney or so I thought. She didn't give a damn about the misery I endured at home. Tonight would be the night that changed my life forever. The day he would come and strip me of my innocence. Every night he'd come into my room, to kiss me good night. But those visits seemed so unnatural. The things he did, the things he wanted me to do.

"I'm going to teach you to be a woman," he said.

I was only thirteen and was scared shitless of him. I knew what we were doing was wrong, but what was I supposed to do? Yell, kick, and scream? Then he might have killed me, too? I watched him unbutton his pants. I clinched the sheets, feeling a strong, unnerving feeling flow through me. I had never seen a penis before, and I certainly never wanted the first one that I saw be my own father's.

"Touch it, grab it, and hold on to it," he ordered me.

Frozen in fear, I did nothing but look at him until his voice grew louder and with more anger. He took my hand and wrapped it around his penis. I let out cries of sorrow, but he just slapped me and told me to "grow up."

"I'm going to make a woman out of you," he repeated. "This is what makes you a woman. Now lay back as I put this inside you. You're going to be a real woman, not like your mother that selfish bitch."

I begged for my father to stop. I even tried to kick him in the groin, but he punched me in the face and told me again to be a "good girl." I hated my father for conti-nuously taking my innocence away from me. I was never the same after what he did. I cried, screamed, shouted, and pleaded for him to stop. I could feel every piece of my insides ripping apart as my father shoved his six-inch manhood inside of me. I wanted to kill him and vowed to myself that one day I would. I resented my mother secretly for staying with a man who was so drunk, evil, and crazy. I knew, after tonight, that my life would never be the same again. He kissed me on the forehead as he fastened his pants to get ready to leave.

"Remember, Danielle, if you tell anyone, they'll never believe you. They'll just say you're lying," he stated as he walked out.

The next week I was in the shower getting ready for school. My mother was again not home. I heard the door open, and I knew it could only be one person...Warrington. First, I heard him flushing the toilet. Then, he pulled back the shower curtain. I turned around, instantly embarrassed. I tried to reach for a towel, but he stopped me. He ran his hands down my breasts and touched my behind. I was scared out of my mind because nowhere in my right mind could this ever be appropriate. He smiled and began to get undressed.

"No, no. Don't get out. I'm coming in," he said.

"Daddy, what are you doing here? I'm taking a shower. I'm naked," I cried out as the warm water cascaded down the skin of my back.

"I know, honey. I want to join. Don't worry. I won't hurt you. I just want to make you feel good."

He joined me in the shower, and I tried to take a step back as far as I could. But the further I went, the closer he got. I stood there frozen in fear as his hands touched all over my body. He kissed my neck as his fingers entered my vagina. I motioned for him to stop, but again he slapped me across the face. I cried as his penis replaced his fingers inside me. Why did I have to endure this torture every single damn day? What was wrong with this man? Why wasn't my mother ever home? I grew disgusted as I heard Warrington telling me how good I made him feel.

He finally got out of the shower, dressed, and left the bathroom. I turned the water off and cried for a good twenty minutes. I put on my clothes and ran out the door to head to school. I wanted to run away from home. I had to. This was absolutely no way for a teenager to live.

Later that night, my mother was absent. Where the hell was she? What kind of mother abandons her daughter like this? I wondered. She's never home with me. It made me wonder if she even cared about me anymore. After we ate the dinner that I prepared for him, he ordered me to wash the dishes, then join him in the bedroom. I boldly told him no. This was surely not the answer he was expecting because the next thing I knew, I was greeted with a punch to the eye that landed me on the floor. I tried to get away as I scooted on the floor toward the living room. Warrington ran after me, took off his belt, and began whooping me like a slave. This man was pure evil, and there was no way to stop him. I finally broke free and ran upstairs to my bedroom. I slammed the door shut and heard him banging on it. I hid in my closest like a child hiding from a monster she had seen under her bed.

"Open the door, Danielle. Danielle, I'm only going to tell you one more time. Open this door before I break it down."

I continued hiding in the closest. I heard him banging on the door again as if he was slamming his body against it. I knew it'd only be a matter of time before he would break into my room. I prayed for God to help me. Just to make it all go away. Tears rolled down my cheeks like a rainstorm. Finally, he busted through, looking for me. He opened the closet door, yanked me out, and threw me onto the bed. He whipped me a few more times with his belt before he tried to touch me again. He told me this was my punishment. Every day I didn't satisfy him, I would get whipped because I was his slave, and he was my master.

Chapter 2

No One Would Listen

It was almost two years later before I found the courage to tell someone what was going on between my father and me. I finally decided I would tell my mother. Surely, a good mother would stick up and support her child, right? Hmmph, or so I thought, I found my mother working on some files buried on her desk, while tapping a computer keyboard in front of her. Slowly, I approached her with what was the hardest confession I ever had to make.

"Mom, can I talk to you about something?" I asked, standing in front of her.

"Ugh, Danielle, is this important? Don't you see I'm busy?" she replied with an attitude.

"It's about Dad."

"What about him?" she questioned, annoyed as her fingers tapped the keyboard and eyes still gazed at the computer screen.

"Well," I said, clearing my throat. "When you are at work, Dad does things to me," I admitted.

"Does what things to you?" she asked, not batting one eye.

"He does things to me...that he should be doing to you."

As quickly as the words poured out from underneath my tongue, my mother finally took her eyes away from the computer screen. That did it. That was what got her attention. I just knew she would come rescue me from the dark hell I felt I was in.

"You lying bitch!"

"What?"

"Always trying to seek attention. Now if you don't mind, I am very busy, Dani."

"I'm not lying," I yelled as tears rolled down my cheeks. "He does this every night that you are gone. If you don't believe me, ask him, ask him, Momma!" I painfully cried out as I tried hard to make this woman who gave me life believe me.

"Okay, Danielle. What does he do to you?"

"He used to make me touch his penis, and, then as I got older, he would come into my room at night while you were at work and have sex with me. I begged him to stop, but he would just slap me across the face and tell me to be quiet. Please, Mom, leave this man. I beg of you.

For my sake?" I pleaded with this woman to be a responsible woman and mother, to do the right thing.

"How long has this been going on?"

"For two years," I answered.

"For two years? Why the hell didn't you say anything before?"

"I was too scared. He told me not to tell you, but I am tired of this. He is my father. I am only fifteen years old. This is not right, Mom. If you don't believe me, ask him."

My father had just walked through the door, which meant soon it would be time for my mother to leave but not before we finally got to the bottom of this. I had hoped my mother would put him in his place. I was hoping his place would be on the corner of Woodward and 6 Mile. My mother and I walked into the living room where my father was drinking a can of beer and staring out the window.

"Hello, Warrington. You got a minute? I need to talk to you about something," my mother said to my father.

"Um, sure, what's going on?"

I waited in the kitchen while my parents talked. I didn't want to feel the awkward tension in the room. The conversation didn't last long because, the next thing I knew, my mother called out to me.

"Danielle Latrice Turner, get in here right now!"

"Yes, mother," I said, as I entered the living room, but, before I could figure out what was going on, I was greeted with a hard slap across the face. I broke out in tears as I grabbed my stinging face.

"What the hell did I tell you about lying, Danielle? Now he tells me, you're going around being fast with boys at school, and you wanted to cover it up before you got into trouble. Well, Danielle, I have no damn tolerance for this nonsense. You brought this on yourself. Stop lying. Are you acting out for attention or something? I'm leaving for work now. I swear, girl, I just don't know what's wrong with you."

"Mom, I'm not lying, and I'm not messing with any boys at school. Mama, please believe me," I begged.

"Danielle, that's enough!" my father interjected.

I looked at him and rolled my eyes with anger. How dare he say I am lying? He was the cause of all of my pain. My mother grabbed her briefcase, gave me a disapproving stare, and walked out the door. I tried to run out after her.

"Mom, please don't leave me alone with him. I beg you. Please stay home today."

"Danielle, please get yourself back in the house."

I watched her drive off in her car as I stood on the porch too afraid of what to do next. I tried to sneak away down the street, but, before I hit the stairs, my father called me back into the house. *Oh, no,* I thought. Going against my gut feeling, I went back inside. I should've kept walking. He told me to shut the door behind me. His eyes were stern, and I could tell he was furious that I had told Mom about our dirty, little secret.

"Didn't I tell you not to tell anyone about our secret?" he questioned, frustrated. "Didn't I?" he repeated.

"Yes..." I answered as my father hit me so hard across the face I fell to the floor.

"I'm going to teach you a hard lesson about keeping secrets," he said.

I watched him take off his belt. I tried to make a run for it and lock myself in my bedroom, but my father caught me halfway up the stairs. He dragged me into my parent's bedroom and locked the door. He shoved me onto the bed and told me he was going to make me pay for telling on him. He pulled down my pants, and forced himself inside of me from behind. I let out small wails of agony and pain. My father was relentless when it came to destroying the purity I was supposed to have. I was only fifteen, and already had the sexual capacity of a grown woman. I hated my parents. I don't know why my mother didn't stick up for me. It was almost as if she knew what was going on between us but didn't care. I hated my father for raping me and because he would rather torture me instead of sticking his dick inside of some other older woman. My parents were two messed-up individuals. But why did my life have to suffer for it?

Today I have decided to take back my life, I thought. I had told my mother, and she had done nothing. There was no way on God's green earth that I would allow this to continue. I'm ending this once and for all. By any means necessary. Danielle Latrice Turner is getting the little piece of happiness they took from me. My father is going to pay for being a sick and mentally disturbed pervert, if it's the last damn thing I do.

He finally tired himself out and collapsed on the bed, falling asleep. The sick bastard. I got myself together and quietly left the room as my silent cries shielded the pain I felt inside, but not before I grabbed one little thing from on top of the closest shelf. I unlocked the door as he laid in the bed, knocked out. I left with something that I knew was going to help me get my life back.

Chapter 3

Planning My Escape

I decided...I finally decided that my life couldn't continue on like this. Again, my mother was not at home. She was at work, as usual. I swear she must've had a family on the side because she was never home with us or, better yet, with me. I walked into my room and placed my father's gun inside of a drawer. I locked it away, so it would be waiting for me when I got home. This man was going to learn his lesson one way or the other. I wasn't having it anymore. I couldn't spend the rest of my life being his whore.

I grabbed my backpack and keys and snuck out the house to school unnoticed. School had slowly become my sanctuary, my getaway from the bullshit I was forced to come home to. My home life slowly started to bother me because of the fucked-up mess I had to deal with. I couldn't even concentrate on schoolwork. I had bigger issues, and passing classes stopped becoming a concern to me; sadly enough though, my teachers began to notice.

I was sitting in Ms. Folsom's English class as she was collecting homework. She stopped to look at me when she saw that I was empty-handed.

"Danielle, did you do your homework?"

"Nope," I replied confidently yet annoyed.

"Danielle, this is the fourth time you've missed a homework assignment. Are you trying to fail this class purposely?" she questioned.

"If it's my fourth time, then you still shouldn't be surprised. You're the one who keeps asking just to get disappointed."

I rolled my eyes to hide the pain I felt because inside I was embarrassed. But what was I supposed to do...tell her that every night, when I go home, my father used my pussy as his own personal playground for his dick. I think not. This white lady wouldn't know what to do if I told her some mess like that.

"Ms. Turner, I'm going to have to have a meeting with your parents to see what's going on with you. Stay after class. I don't know what happened. You used to be such a good student."

"I'm sixteen. Who still has parent-teacher conferences with teenagers? I'm not ten," I shouted out as everybody but Ms. Folsom laughed at my smart-ass remark.

She was clearly disappointed with me as she frowned but continued on with her lesson plan for the day. The structure of how to write a perfect essay was what she taught. But all I could think about was getting my life back. No normal sixteen-year-old should endure pain like this. At the end of the hour, Ms. Folsom closed the door and sat one seat in front of me, with her hands placed on top of one another, staring at me.

"What?" I replied with a twist in my lip.

"What is going on with you? At the beginning, you were one of my brightest students. Now I don't know who you are," Ms. Folsom said. "Is there anything going on at home?"

I wanted to yell, "YES! My father molests me!" I thought about telling her, but then, because I was a minor, the school would contact either a social worker or, even worse, Child Protective Services. Then that would just create even bigger problems at home. So I lied.

"No, nothing is going on at home. Can I go now please?"

"I still want to speak to your parents about your missing homework assignments."

"My mother works all of the time, and my father comes home when I leave, so I really don't know who you could talk to. It's really not that a big of a deal, Ms. Folsom. I turned in the homework assignment before you got in, you just didn't see it."

"Dammit, you're going to fail my class, Danielle. I know you are smarter than this," she yelled, slapping her hand on the desk. She removed her glasses and wiped her nose.

"I don't know what you want from me. Can I go please?" I pleaded, trying my hardest to get this agony over with.

She gave me a progress report to give to my parents and let me continue on my way. Now with my mood ruined, I decided to skip the rest of my classes for the day.I headed home to work on getting my plan together.

When I got home, I was lucky; nobody was home. Most importantly, my father wasn't home. So I decided to pack my clothes in my suitcase. I didn't exactly know where I was going, but I did know where the hell I wasn't. I wasn't about to stay here and get abused any longer. Just as I got halfway down the stairs, I saw my father walking through the door. I thought, *DAMN!* as he hung up his jacket on the coat rack and turned to look at me.

"Danielle, what the hell are you doing home so damn early? Why aren't you in school, and just where the hell do you think you're going?" my father questioned me sternly.

I stood frozen in fear. All I could do was come up with a quick lie.

"Um, I'm going over to a friend's house for the weekend. We had a half a day of school today."

"Where are you going with all your bags packed for the weekend? You going to a boy's house, aren't you?"

"No, Dad. I'm going to see Jasmyn. She's my best friend."

"You gonna walk all the way to her house with your suitcases? What did I tell you about lying to me, Danielle?"

"I'm not lying to you, Daddy."

"You're lying to me right now! I told you that I can't stand to be lied to. You're lying to me and cutting school. What the hell is wrong with you?" he hollered as he took off after me.

I dropped my luggage and ran up the stairs toward my bedroom. I was almost there when he dragged me into the room and threw me onto the bed. He landed a punch across my face. I pleaded with my father to let me go, but he just told me to shut up.

"You think it's okay to lie to me and try to sneak out the house?" he said as he wrapped his hands around my throat. I grasped at his hands, trying to loosen their grip. I, also, tried to kick him off me. That was when he began to tug at my jeans, and I knew what would soon follow. He slowly pulled his slacks down and told me to get undressed. I kicked him in the stomach, and he reacted by punching me in the jaw. As I was holding my face, he pulled off my jeans and underwear. I screamed loudly for someone to help me, but, as usual, my cries went unheard. I closed my eyes as I felt him enter me. The smell of his breath as his body was pressed against mine reeked of cheap liquor. My father was an avid drinker. So there was no doubt that he had had a few shots of either tequila or E&J. What was wrong with him mentality? What the hell would possess a man to sleep with his own child? He was a sick, sadistic bastard, and somehow this torture had to end. I continued to tell him to stop as he ignored my cries. I saw my mother step in from within the hallway. I just knew that she would put a stop to all of this. I motioned for my mother to come. To ask what the hell are you doing to my daughter? Maybe even put a bullet in his back. But what she did was something I would've never imagined from her. She stood in the doorway for a minute or two.

"Mommy, help me, help me please! Make him stop!"

All she did was place her index finger over her pressed lips to hush me and then stepped out of the doorway and shut the door. *What type of shit is this? My mother stood by and did nothing. What kind of father rapes and molests his daughter, but worse, what kind of mother stands by and lets it happen?*

From that moment, I knew neither of my parents gave a damn about me. If I wanted to escape this hell, I would have to take matters into my own hands. After my father grew tired of using me as his cheap, whored-out prostitute, he got dressed. I got up and searched around the house for my mother. Calling out to her, but she was nowhere to be found.

"She's gone. Like always, she's gone. It's just me and you here in this house, baby girl. Now go in that kitchen and fix my dinner," my father ordered.

He went downstairs and sat on the couch, watching TV and opening a can of beer. It was going to be a long night, and it was either going to be me or him. *I'm tired of being his victim, tired of being his whore, slut, and trick, whatever the hell you wanted to call it. I'm not his damn wife. Shouldn't he be making me dinner?* I sat in my bedroom, ignoring his requests to prepare his food. I stared at the wall, stewing in my own frustration. He yelled out to me again. And again, I ignored him. I wasn't going to do shit for this man. He wasn't even a man. *What man gets off by sleeping with his daughter?* I locked my eyes to the drawer where I had kept that gun hidden. I needed to protect myself against Satan. I was in hell, and there was only one way out of this place.

My father must've grown tired of me ignoring his demands. He busted into my room, slamming the doors and shoving me against the wall.

"Didn't you hear me calling you, woman? Get your ass down stairs and fix my plate!"

"I'm not your wife. I'm your daughter. I'm not doing this anymore. Stay away from me! Please!" I cried out.

"Shut up!" he yelled, slapping me across the face so hard that I fell to the floor.

"Now you listen to me. You're going to do whatever the hell I tell you to do. Do you understand me? I run this house, not you little girl. You don't have anywhere else to go. So I suggest you get used to being my little bitch. Now get your ass downstairs, before I break your damn neck."

I couldn't take it anymore. I had put up with being molested for three years, and neither of my parents had done a damn thing about it. No one loved me. No one cared about me. So this meant I had to care about myself. I watched my father walk out my room. As I followed him down to the kitchen, I began preparing his dinner but not without a plan to get back at this man for all the awful shit he had done to me. I hated Warrington with everything in me. The nerve of him, he was so damned demanding. Screwing me one minute and then wanting me to cook him food the next. If I was being treated like a

wife, then just what the hell was my mother doing for
him? Something wasn't right with this picture. I began
cooking baked chicken, string beans, and Jambalaya. As I
placed the chicken in the oven, I heard my father yell out
to me again.

"Danielle, are you done cooking my damn food yet?
Hurry the fuck up. I'm hungry," my father hollered.

I tried to tolerate my father's orders, but it was
becoming just too much for me to bear, and I broke down
crying. I felt so weak because there was nothing I could
do to get out of this. Suddenly, it dawned on me that my
father took pills with his food. I thought, *I have to leave
this house if I want a shot at a better life*. I replaced his
medication with sleeping pills. I gave him just enough to
knock him out for the night to make my escape. Finally, I
finished his dinner and brought it out to him. He rolled
his eyes at me as he began to dig into his plate.

"Took you long enough…where's my back medication? We do this every day, Danielle. Stop acting like
you're new at this."

"Then next time get your shit your damn self," I
replied under my breath.

"What did you say, little girl?"

"I'm not a little girl! I'm almost an adult. Stop doing
this to me."

"Girl, hush! Come sit down next to me and watch TV. No one is doing anything to you. Just sit down and keep me company. I'm down here all lonely," he said as he turned on an old episode of *Friends*.

He pulled my arm to sit down next to him. While he ate his food, he constantly took shots at me. He took his hand and rubbed it up and down my thigh.

"Why don't you take your medicine now? Don't you think it's time to take your pills?" I persuaded him.

"Oh, yeah, yeah, I almost forgot. You always know how to take care of me. I need to keep you around all the time."

"But you can't. I'm not your wife. I'm your daughter."

"Girl, hush and hand me my damn pills. You know your damn place."

I handed him a couple of sleeping pills that he thought were for his back pain. I just couldn't wait until they went into effect. I was going to run out of there so fast. This man was relentless at making my life miserable.

"Go in the kitchen and get me some more damn food. You know this isn't enough to fill me up. What are you trying to do? Starve me to death?" he said, frustrated.

I rolled my eyes and grabbed his plate. I walked back to the kitchen, wishing I had some poison to sprinkle into his food. There was hardly any dinner left for me, yet he had asked for more. He didn't give a damn whether I ate or not.

"Danielle! Hurry up, girl! What you doing in there?" he hollered from the other room.

"I'm coming! Damn!" I answered. I replenished his plate and slammed it down on his tray.

"What the hell is wrong with you? You better check your attitude." He pulled my arm to get me to sit down next to him.

After about twenty minutes or so, he was slowly starting to show the effects of the drug. I sprinted upstairs to my room and gathered my belongings. I put them into my suitcase, grabbed my phone, and ran out the house. Where was I going from this point on? I had no clue. I was a free woman who no longer had to worry about being beaten and molested by her father. Where was my mother? I did not know. But the train of misery was over, or so I thought. Or better yet, one began right after one ended. It was time to start a new life, and I was anxious to see what was out there waiting for me.

Chapter 4

Run Away, Love, Run Away

I had been walking the ten and a half blocks to my friend Jasmyn's house in the bitter Detroit cold. I knew Jasmyn would be up because her parents usually worked midnight shifts, so she was pretty much a night owl. This was the perfect opportunity for me, because I needed somewhere to rest to get away from the all the craziness that was running through my head. I just knew, as I heard the faint sounds of a police siren, that someone would find me out. *I hope the sleeping pills I gave him don't kill him. I'm too afraid to tell anyone. How can I explain that my father has molested me almost every night for the past three years and that I drugged him to rid myself of the horror? Naw, I can't tell anyone. If things catch up with me, I'd just say it was a simple mistake. Better yet, I'd say he tried to commit suicide. I'm sure my mother will probably never come back anyway.*

I made my way to her front porch and could barely raise my hand to knock on the door. Both my hands were frozen stiff from this cold air. I stood there trying to warm myself up. December winters in Detroit were no joke. I began to call out to her with hopes that she would hear me.

"Hey, Jasmyn! Hey, Jas-myn! Open the door!"

A few moments later, I could hear the locks turn, and Jasmyn appeared in the doorway with purple silk pajamas on. Her parents always spoiled her. She was always given the best — the best clothes, shoes, education. I could tell her parents truly loved her. Often times, it made me jealous. But Jasmyn was a good friend to me. So I knew she would never flaunt her parent's wealth and affection in my face.

Jasmyn nudged me a little to get my attention from the trance I must've been in. Her caramel skin shone brightly against the fluorescent lights within her home.

"Danielle, it's almost ten o'clock at night. Why aren't you at home, and why the heck are you hollering? We got neighbors, you know?"

"I know…I know. I just really need to come in. Please, it's freezing out here, girl," I said, shivering.

"Yeah, yeah, come in. I'll make you some hot chocolate. I was watching an episode of *Criminal Minds* on CBS. It just came on. I think that Shemar Moore is sexy. You look a mess. Do you want to talk about it?"

"I...can't talk about it. It's just...I can't... Oh-my-gawd, I can't talk about it. It's my father. He's just been making living with him so unbearable."

"What? What happened? Can you talk about it?"

I just shook my head. I couldn't stand there and tell her I was getting raped by my own father.

"Are you sure you don't want to talk about it because you look like there's a lot on your mind?" Jasmyn questioned me.

"Yeah, I'm sure," I said, shaking my head. "I had a long day. I really just want to rest and lay my head down. I got a lot going on right now."

"Sure, sure, um, let me straighten up the extra room for you. I'll get a pillow and blanket for you. Just make yourself at home, homegirl."

"Thanks, Jasmyn, I really appreciate it. Thanks for looking out for me."

I followed Jasmyn to the extra room and helped her set it up. Once she stepped out of the room, I closed the door behind me and fell on the bed. I was exhausted after everything I had gone through. It was hard to sleep, but I found a way to shut my eyes to try to forget about the unpleasantness of the day, or hell, the unpleasantness that was my life.

The next day, I hadn't even realized how late it was, or even the fact that Jasmyn's parents had come home. I was turning over in the bed and was surprised when I was awakened by Monica, Jasmyn's mother.

"What are you doing sleeping in our bed? When did you come over, Danielle? We didn't tell Jasmyn she could have company. Do your parents know you slept over here?"

"No, ma'am. I came over last night," I replied.

"Jasmyn! Get in here! Can you explain why Danielle is in our home when I specifically told you no company?"

"Mom, you act as if I snuck a boy into the house. This is my best friend. She's been having it pretty rough at home lately. I was just letting her crash here for the night. What's wrong with that? She had no other place to go?" Jasmyn stated in my defense.

"Well, I'm sorry about your home life but don't get too comfortable here. My home isn't a hotel. I expect you to find somewhere to go by the end of the night," Jasmyn's mom said.

"Mom!"

"No, it's all right, Jas. Don't worry about it. I'll find somewhere to go, maybe an aunt or something."

"See, problem solved. Now, Jasmyn, I expect you and your friend to be on your way to school. You're going to be late."

"Mom, why can't she just stay with us? She is having a really hard time right now."

"I have already made my decision. There is no room with your brother Jonathan about to come home from college. Plus, I don't want someone like her in our home," she whispered quietly to her daughter as she left the room. Jasmyn then turned and looked over to me.

"Where are you going to go, Danielle? You have no other place to go. You're gonna be homeless sleeping on the streets. It's the middle of December in Detroit. It's too damn cold to be outside and with all these crazy-ass people."

"You're crazy, Jas," I replied as I laughed at her comment about crazy fools in the D.

"I'll be all right. I'm a strong girl. I'll be okay. I can probably call a family member or something. I'll be okay. Thanks anyway. Let's just head to school."

We grabbed our backpacks and headed out the door.

Chapter 5

Secrets and Lies

Later that evening as I tried to brave the bitter Detroit cold, I realized there was no way in hell I could make it through the night. I had to call someone and the only person I could think of was my aunt Tralene. See now my Aunt Tralene was the blunt and bossy all up in your face, and tell it like it is type. She had a real snooty daughter, my cousin Sadie. She was supposed to go on to school to be a doctor or lawyer or some shit. I didn't really care. All I knew right now was I needed somewhere to stay and my parent's house, nor the cold-ass concrete, were a good choice.

Finally arriving at my aunt's home, I noticed how nicely it was kept. It was nowhere near as fancy as Jasmyn's home. But I could feel the love in the home by the pictures hung up of her and my cousin. Even an old photo of her late husband who had died in the Gulf War was sitting in the middle of the mantle right above the fireplace. I took a seat on the freshly worn black leather couch. I was exhausted. I was interrupted by my aunt who was standing in front of me puffing a cigarette.

"Now tell me again. Why you don't want to go home? What's going on?"

"It's just not safe for me to live there anymore."

"Girl, what in the world is you talking about?" she questioned as she took a seat in a huge black recliner.

She was short and petite, so her legs didn't quite reach the floor when she reclined the chair.

"Well, I never told anyone this, and it's pretty hard to confess. I'm sure you won't believe me, but…ever since I was thirteen, my father has been molesting me. He's been forcing himself on to me. You know…having sex with me almost every night. When I told my mother, I thought she would kill him or something, but she just called me a lying bitch. Even when she caught him in the act, all she did was tell me to be quiet! What the hell kind of mother is that?" I broke down crying. "I feel as if she puts her job as a district attorney ahead of being a mother to me. She is always rushing off to leave in the evening. My parents are horrible. Please I can't go back there."

"Why didn't you go to the police? And what job as a district attorney? Your mother never worked as a DA. Your mother never even made it past her second year of college," my aunt commented.

"What are you talking about, Aunt Tralene?" I questioned suspiciously. "She's always leaving in the evening, coming home in the morning or middle of the day. I know she has a job."

"Last time I checked, your mother was still high up on that hoe stroll over on Woodward and 6 Mile."

"You're lying. Stop talking bad about my mother."

"I'm not. I'm telling you the truth. That's why she's never been around much. Your mother is a drugged-up prostitute who let your step-father come in, raise you, and molest you in order to support her drug habit. The two of them came up with this crazy-ass story, so you wouldn't think otherwise."

"Step-father?" I asked, confused.

"Warrington Hall is not your biological father. Your real father walked out on your mother long ago, when you were little."

"I don't believe you. Stop lying. I know you're lying." I yelled, as I broke down in tears and dropped to the floor.

I couldn't believe what I was hearing. I placed my hands over my ears in disbelief. My aunt pulled me up from the floor and tried to console me. I broke free, ran to the bathroom, and locked the door behind me. *I can't believe that my whole entire life has been a lie, a fucking lie. This can't be happening right now. Why would my aunt try to hurt me like this? The man I've always thought of as my father isn't. My mother allowed a complete stranger to come in and molest me.* I was beyond devastated. I didn't know what to do. I had to find out the truth. I pulled my cell phone out of my pocket and tried to call my mother. I couldn't believe she picked up after the second ring.

"Hello… Mom?"

"Where are you?" she questioned.

"I'm at Aunt Tralene's house. Ma, tell me the truth. Is Warrington Hall really my father?"

"What are you talking about? Of course he is. He raised you, didn't he?"

"Mom, don't lie to me. I know you're not a DA."

"Of course I'm not. I never said I was. Look, Dani, I have to get going soon. I'm about to go. I got to make my quota for tonight or somebody's coming for me," she quickly said before hanging up in my ear.

I was at a true loss for words. My whole life had been a complete lie. I stared at my reflection in the mirror and wondered who I was. I wondered who my parents were because apparently everything I thought was a sad untruth. Breaking my thoughts, I heard my aunt Tralene knocking on the door.

"Come on out, Danielle. I know you're hurting, sweetheart. But locking yourself in the bathroom isn't going to help."

I wiped the tears off my sandy brown face and ran my fingers through my long hair and opened the door.

"Hey, honey. I'm sorry. Maybe I should've kept things to myself," my aunt said as she placed her arms around me and walked me to my new bedroom.

"No, I wish someone would've told me sooner."

I sat down on the bed and wondered what to do next.

"Everything will be just fine. You get some rest. I'll get started preparing dinner. Your cousin Sadie will be home soon," she said as she gave me a hug and a quick peck on the forehead and shut the door behind her.

I laid down on the bed and contemplated what I would do. What kind of drama would follow me now? It was always something. One thing after another, first, my father molested me and my mother didn't step in to help. Now, my father really wasn't my father but some damn stranger who had fucked me more times than I could count. As far as my mother, she did God knows what, with God knew who. What kind of mother allowed her daughter to be molested by some dick just so he could support her? Did she have some kind of excessive drug habit? This was a huge pill to swallow, and I felt as I if I was truly getting fucked in more ways than one. Little did I know that this was only the beginning.

Chapter 6

Desmond Little

I t had been a few months since I had settled in with my aunt Tralene. After everything I had been through with my parents, I knew I wasn't going back there again. I couldn't go back there again. My aunt did everything she possibly could to make her house feel like a home for me. She cooked, cleaned, and even listened to me as I discussed the incidents with my "step-father." I slowly became adjusted to living with my pompous, stuck-up, snotty, and know-it-all cousin Sadie.

Sadie was about 5'7" with fair skin and a Halle Berry styled haircut. She could have been a model with her petite structure but nope, she decided that, upon finishing high school, she would attend Wayne State University for their medical program. She was going to be a doctor. I really didn't care about her bougie career plans. I never really thought ahead as to what to do for college. Hell, I just wanted to finish high school.

I was in the middle of watching a TV program when my cousin walked in the room. She looked upset as she stood in front of me with her hands on her hips pouting and tapping her foot.

"What are you doing just lying in the bed? Aren't you going to get up and do something? You've been lying in bed all day. My goodness, you're so lazy!" she said as she shook her head in disbelief.

"Sadie, it's Saturday. We don't have school today. Take a chill pill. These are the only two days we can sit around and be lazy."

"Yeah, well, maybe for you, but I'm heading down to Harper Hospital to do my volunteering with the elderly. You should do some volunteer work. Might do you some good. Plus, it looks really good on your college applications. You are planning on going to college, aren't you?" she questioned with a snotty, judgmental look upon her face.

"I don't know, Sadie. I'm only sixteen. You're seventeen. I have a whole year to decide if I'm going."

"Are you serious? Ugh, how are we related? I knew in junior high I was going to college, the school, and what for. I just have things prepared like that. I sure hope you don't waste your day away watching television. It's so counterproductive. All right. Well, I'm off to the hospital," she said finally leaving my damn room.

It was definitely an adjustment living with her. She had been up since seven in the morning, getting ready to go do some volunteer work. I just didn't understand the point of it. I could definitely tell that we were raised by two different women who were in two completely different states of mind. I didn't like going to school, let alone, offering my free time to feed Jell-O to some old-ass people. I found the remote and turned on my favorite VH1 program. This was how I planned to spend my Saturday.

****

I walked into my aunt's house after another boring day at school. I threw my book bag on the recliner chair and plopped on the couch. I was beyond sleepy. I reached for the remote and turned on the TV. My aunt was talking in the distance, like she was on the phone in the back room. I didn't begin to pay attention until I heard her say my name. I walked over to where her bedroom was and listened outside the door. She was having a conversation with someone. I just couldn't pinpoint who it was at first.

"But this is your daughter. I'm still raising mine. You need to be there for that girl." I overheard her say. If it wasn't for her using speakerphone, I wouldn't have known she was talking to my trifling mother.

"Look, she obviously doesn't want to live with us anymore. So maybe living with you is best for her. Quite frankly, I'm done being a mother. Hell, she is sixteen years old; she's grown. She'll be all right," my mother said.

"This is your daughter you're talking about. How can you give up on your own child, just because you're tired of her?"

"Danielle is not a child, and I just don't want to do it anymore. Truth be told, I never really wanted her anyway. She messed up my life, but now that she's grown, I can get back to living again."

"You don't want to raise Danielle! You know you really are a sorry excuse for a mother. That girl has been through a lot. You should've gotten that child into some counseling. Seriously, Cheryl, how could you just allow someone to molest your own child and you sit back and do nothing? What kind of mother does that?" I heard my aunt question my mother.

Oh, no, I thought, *I think that was supposed to have remained a secret.*

"What...Danielle was never molested? No one ever touched that girl! She is a damn lie, Tralene. That's what I'm talking about. That girl is always lying. I don't know what to do with her. Danielle is a lying bitch who has ruined the hell out of my life. She caused my man to walk out on me. Her own father didn't want her ass. What makes you think I want her? Come on. I'm better off now that she's gone. I am finally free. I was only with Warrington's controlling ass to support Danielle, and now that she is living with you, I can finally live my life the way I want to. I don't give a damn what you say or think. I'm a grown-ass woman, and I can do whatever the hell I damn well please. I've told you time and time again that I'm not cut out to be someone's mother. I never was. I don't care if I ever see Danielle again. Good riddance to her. Now, are you done because I have things to do and men waiting on me? I have to go."

When my mother ended the conversation with my aunt, I just let out a small cry. I couldn't believe what I heard my aunt and mother say. What was this mess about my mother not wanting me? My mother was a complete bitch for what she had said. *I ruined her life?* And how could she just lie to my aunt and say I had never been molested? She walked in on my step-father having sex with me and didn't do a damn thing. I hated that woman. She should've given me up for adoption because, at least then, I would've had a good chance for a better life.

Feeling a little confused and frustrated, I made my way back into the living room. I could hear my aunt open her bedroom door and walk down the hallway. Apparently, she felt sorry for me because this was the sweetest I had ever heard her speak to me.

"Hello, Danielle sweetie," she said as she entered the room. "How are you? How is school going? Can I ask you a question? And will you answer it honestly please? I won't get mad," my aunt said.

"Yeah, what is it?" I replied, annoyed.

"Did your father ever touch you in any places that weren't appropriate while you were at home?"

"I thought we'd already discussed this?"

"I know. It's just that your mother is telling me something different. That's all."

At that moment, I completely lost it. How in the hell could my mother lie like that? She had witnessed the shit herself.

"Well, to be honest and with no disrespect to you, to hell with my mother. That woman stood by and did nothing for three years while my father came home drunk and used me like a cheap-ass prostitute. She even walked in as that man violated me, and, as I yelled out to her for help, she did nothing! She did nothing! She basically told me to be quiet and take it. What kind of mother does that?" I yelled as I tried my best to hold back the waterfall of tears trying to stream down my cheeks as I relived those horrific nights. "Now she doesn't want to be my mother anymore. She doesn't want to be there for me. Then to hell with her. I don't need her. That woman has never taken responsibility for me in the last sixteen years."

I stood staring out the window. I could feel my heart beating fast and my breath shortening. I was just devastated. I couldn't believe this was how my life was turning out to be. At age sixteen, I had been molested, abandoned, and lied to. *Why would God allow me to go through this hell?* I've prayed for God to take me away from this misery, but He never did. He allowed me to constantly be raped and robbed of my innocence for three years. So from this moment on, I had no belief in God. God would forever be a stranger to me. He ignored me, so I refuse to put my faith into something that didn't exist.

My aunt placed her arm around my shoulders to console me, but there wasn't a damn thing she could say or do which could take my pain away.

"I know you're hurting right now, Danielle. You've been through a lot. Just know that your mother was not in a good place when you were living with her. That's why she has asked me to take on the responsibilities of raising you. She believes this will be the best place for you," my aunt told me.

I turned to her and rolled my eyes. I knew it was a lie. I knew my mother hadn't told her that.

"Bullshit! That's complete bullshit!"

"Danielle, watch your language!" my aunt warned.

"Why? Let's keep things honest. My mother doesn't want me anymore because I don't fit into her perfect little lifestyle, and she figures that, since you've done such a good job raising Sadie, you could do a good job raising Danielle. Only thing is, Danielle don't need anybody to raise her. She said I'm grown, right?" I said with a major attitude.

I grabbed my book bag and the house key and made my way out the door. At that point, I didn't give a damn about anybody but myself.

"Danielle, where the hell are you going?" my aunt called out to me.

"Out…I'll be back."

"Girl, it's almost seven o'clock. You now it's not safe this time of night. Get back in here!" she ordered.

"Why? I'll be okay. I know how to look out for myself. Besides, ain't like I'll amount to anything special like Sadie." I shrugged as I walked out of the door.

I turned down the corner, not knowing just where the hell I was going, but I knew I couldn't stay at that house. I couldn't stay with anybody in my family. Sad thing is, I had nowhere else to live. I was beginning to get hungry, so I decided to walk in to Toni's Party Liquor store. The store was jumping with its usual crowds of teens, drunks, druggies, and late-night partygoers. I pushed past this guy who appeared to have not showered in days. He smiled a toothless grin as he hugged a bottle of gin in his arms. Clearly, he had let life defeat him. After I paid for my BBQ Lays and Hawaiian Punch, I spotted a group of kids from my school standing outside the store. One of them called my name, so I made my way over to them. This was when I laid eyes on the finest guy I had ever seen. He was a popular student at my school. This guy was around 6'2". He had a dark chocolate brown complexion, deep brown eyes, and a smile that melted my heart. All the girls wanted him, so I couldn't imagine why he would want to talk to me.

"Yes," I said shyly.

"Hey, what's your name? I think I know you from school," the guy said to me in a sexy, masculine voice that made me blush.

"Yeah, my name is Danielle."

"Oh, cool. My name is Desmond."

"I know who you are. Everybody knows who you are."

"Yeah, I guess you're right. These are my friends. We were about to head over to St. Andrews. Do you want to go?"

"That's a club, right?" I questioned nervously.

"Uh, yeah, what you scared? You never been to a club? Trust me. It'll be fun. The night will be on me. I'll take care of you. Come on. Don't tell me you got a curfew or something."

"Naw, I don't. I've just never been there before."

"Don't worry. You'll love it."

"Where is it?"

"Downtown on Congress. Stop worrying. Let's go!" he said as we all headed over to Desmond's 2009 Honda Civic. I had to admit, I felt like I was the shit at this moment. The finest guy in the school had insisted that I hang out with him and his friends. I was too damn excited. I'd never felt this way because, until now, I had never had a chance to be a normal teenager and do things like hang out with friends or have crushes on boys. *Damn, I'm starting to get a life, an actual fucking life.*

When we arrived at the club, it was packed with young people just like me enjoying themselves and just vibing to the music. A few of Desmond's friends went over to the bar to get a few drinks which left us alone. I instantly felt butterflies as I occasionally peeked over at him as we sat and ordered nachos.

"You want to dance? You do know how to dance right?"

"Of course, come on." I took his hand and led us to the dance floor.

I saw a few girls from school that were beginning to give me dirty looks, but I didn't care. Right now, all I wanted to do was be with Desmond. Being with him helped me forget all the bullshit I had been through the last three years. The way he touched me made me feel so warm inside. This was a completely different feeling from when my father would touch me. It was sickening and traumatic before, but, this time, it felt special. I closed my eyes and imagined that it was just me and him on that crowded dance floor. I knew I didn't want this night to end. I had to see more of this guy. I had to have him in my life.

Later that evening around twelve a.m., I stood outside the club as Desmond and his buddies who I found out were named Trevor, Tony, and Leroy started to dissipate. I was left there with Desmond on the other side of town. He stood next to me, puffing on his cigarette. He offered me one, so I took the cigarette and placed it between my lips and watched as he lit it for me. I coughed as the smoke filled my nostrils and tobacco inflamed my lungs.

"I take it that you ain't a smoker." He laughed.

"First time for everything, huh? It's getting kind of late. I think I need to be heading home now," I suggested as I turned toward a nearby bus stop.

I stood there, shivering and embarrassed, as I waited on the next Woodward bus to come until he pulled me over to face him.

"I know you aren't about to take the bus back home as slow as they run. Not this late at night. Anything might happen to you. Why don't you let me drive you home? I got you here. Let me make sure you get home safe."

I couldn't turn down the opportunity to spend more time with Desmond, so I excitedly said yes and got back inside his car. I gave him directions to my aunt's house, and, as I enjoyed the ride home, the scent of Ralph Lauren's cologne intoxicated the small space we shared. I would catch him giving me the eye as he drove. I just knew that this guy was made for me. With everything that I'd been through, all I wanted was for someone to love me. I was tired of being hurt and abandoned.

We slowly approached my aunt's house, and I noticed he had placed his hand on my knee. I turned to face him just as he leaned over to kiss me. I had never been kissed by anyone. The emotions that ran through me were of a different feeling than those my father gave me. I actually felt butterflies in my stomach. As we broke away from our kiss, he handed me his number on a small piece of paper and insisted that I call him. I promised that I would. Then I exited his car and walked up my aunt's porch to the door. I took out my key and opened the door and found my aunt sitting in the living room in the recliner by the front door. Her eyes met mine, and I could tell that things were about to go bad. I walked past her, trying to get to my room, when she pulled me by the arm and demanded I talk to her.

"Danielle Turner, just where the hell have you been all night?" she yelled.

"I was out."

"Out with whom, Danielle? It's twelve-thirty in the morning. I've never even let Sadie stay out that damn late. How did you get home?" she questioned, all up in my business.

"Why the hell is you all up in my business? Damn!" I attempted to walk past my aunt, but, to my surprise, she reached out and slapped me across the face.

"Danielle, just who do you think you are talking to like that? You need to learn some damn respect."

"Why? No one ever had any for me."

"Who brought you home?"

"A friend," I answered.

"What friend?"

"A friend from school. His name is Desmond. Now can I please go. I'm tired," I stated with a frustrated attitude.

"Danielle, you have a lot of nerve. You little ungrateful brat, here I am trying to make this a nice, comfortable living environment for you. I even offered for you to go to counseling. But here you are, being disrespectful and disobedient, ugh. I don't know what to do with you?"

"Good, I don't need you to do me any favors," I said with an attitude as I marched toward my room.

Chapter 7

A Love Like This

A few weeks had gone past since I started seeing Desmond. I had never had a boyfriend before, but the feeling was completely overwhelming. I finally had someone who loved and cared for me. I'd been searching for that my whole life. Maybe now, things would finally begin to go my way.

This was the happiest I had been in a very long time. It was a damn shame that my own family couldn't be there for me. They were never there for me, and the longer I stayed with Desmond, the more I came to the painful realization that blood wasn't thicker than water. As we watched Jackie Chan and Chris Tucker in *Rush Hour*, I could tell that he was staring at me through the corners of his eyes.

"What are you doing?"

"I'm just admiring your beauty. That's all. You're so different from the other girls." Desmond said as his beautiful brown eyes met mine.

"I'm sure you say that to all the girls."

"Naw, just you, I really like you," he said coyly as he leaned in to kiss me.

This time, things went further than just an innocent kissing. I felt a different feeling than when I was forced to have sex with my sick and disgusting father. I enjoyed Desmond touching and kissing all over me, then undressing me. I felt like a virgin losing her virginity because this was the way that my first time should have been. I couldn't hold back the satisfying feeling I was finally receiving. I never knew sex could feel this wonderful. We might have been young, but he knew exactly what he was doing. My pussy throbbed from the vibration of his dick. I never wanted him to stop. This was the best high. I had found my drug, and it became my new addiction. Over and over, I called out his name as he worked on me, whispering in my ear how much he loved my pussy. He was definitely showing me some new things I had never experienced before.

After he finished fucking the shit out of me, he took one look at me and started planting kisses gently around my navel. The gentle pecks got lower and lower until his tongue entered me and tickled my vaginal walls. I could feel the nipples on my breasts harden as he flicked his tongue back and forth inside of me. He grabbed my legs and placed them around his shoulders. Going deeper inside, I couldn't help but to moan from the incredible job he was doing on me. This was beyond being an addiction to me now. I needed this shit to live.

Chapter 8

A Test of My Fate

I never did get over what my father did to me. There were times when it would still haunt me in my sleep, keep me up, and have me crying at night. I tried to get past it all, put it all behind me, but I didn't see how I could. He was the one who had killed my love inside. He was the one who had stolen my innocence. I had to end the torture that he had constantly put me through year after year. I had to get my life back. I had to find my little piece of happiness. Things were so screwed up, and I just didn't care anymore. At that point in my life, I didn't need school anymore, and, to be quite honest, it really didn't need me either. As long as my aunt continued to believe that every morning when I left the house I was going to go to school, it was cool with me.

I made my way down the street to where Toni's liquor store was to grab me something to eat when I ran into a couple of kids I knew from around the neighborhood. I said, "Hey," and entered the store as they stood in the parking lot, smoking weed and getting high. My aunt tried to tell me that an education would always take me far in life, but, after being molested by my dad for three years and hearing that my mother didn't want me anymore, I didn't really see the big- ass deal about finishing school and doing something special with my life.

I bought some chips and pop and joined the kids in the parking lot.

"Hey, Danielle. What are you doing over here?"

"Nothing. Just chilling. What are y'all doing today? It's three-forty five," I said to DeShawn Taylor, a senior at my school.

"You see what we doing?" he chuckled as the other kid joined in.

DeShawn kind of had a thing for me, but he was nowhere near as fine as Desmond. He was tall and goofy-looking with no real goals or ambitions.

"You want a hit? You ever smoked weed before?" DeShawn's friend asked.

"No," I replied, as he handed me a joint.

"I heard you with Desmond now. That's cool, though. I always thought you were kind of cute. You got a nice ass."

"DeShawn, shut up," I blurted out, as I took a puff of the joint.

I instantly choked as the drug entered my system. It felt like my lungs were on fire. For a moment there, I thought I was going to die.

"Calm down, Danielle. Dang! This your first time. You'll be okay. You got to get used to it," DeShawn assured me.

The next few times I tried it were better than the first. This gave me a high when sex wasn't available. It was a good distraction from all the fucked-up shit going on in my life. It was beginning to get late, so I started walking toward my aunt's house. Unfortunately, it started pouring down raining. I couldn't believe this mess. I was completely soaked, but that wasn't the worst part. As I walked up to my aunt's, I found all of my belongings sitting on the porch. *What the hell is going on? I know she isn't putting me out!* I went in to find out what was going on. I pulled out my house key and tried to open the door, but, for some reason, it didn't work. No matter how many times I placed the key in the door, I just couldn't get it to open. I began to bang on the door and call out to my aunt. I was in shock when my aunt came to the door.

"Aunt Tralene, Aunt Tralene, it's me. Danielle! Open the door," I yelled out.

"Yes, Danielle."

"My key doesn't work, and why is all of my stuff on the porch?"

"Because you don't live here anymore, and I got the locks changed. I did everything I could to make this a home for you, Danielle. I understand that you've been through a lot growing up, but there is no excuse to be consistently disobedient and disrespectful to me and Sadie. I'm sorry. I just can't tolerate you anymore," my aunt confessed to me.

"What? I have nowhere else to go. I can't move back home. What am I supposed to do? I'm sorry. I didn't mean—"

"It's just a little too late for apologies. I tried to be there for you. I offered to pay for counseling. I opened up my home to you. And you repeatedly have shown no remorse for your actions. So, since you believe you don't need anyone, go out there and live life on your own. I honestly don't need you being a bad influence on Sadie. She's going places with her life. She just got accepted to Wayne State University, and she is going to be a pre-med student there in the fall."

"Oh, so that is what this is all about? You're afraid I may come along and ruin your perfect little girl's life? I didn't have the same life as Sadie. I didn't have a mother who gave a damn about me. Even as a single mother, yes, you were still better than my mom. Instead, I had a man who I believed was my father, who fucked me like a prostitute for three years. Nobody gives a damn about

Danielle. So you want me out your life? fine! I'm out of here."

I grabbed my bags and walked off the porch as my aunt slammed the door behind her. I couldn't believe this shit. No one in my family cared enough about me to want to take care of me. Everybody had abandoned me or had given up on me. Now I had no place to go in the middle of this damn rainstorm. It was beginning to get late, a quarter to seven to be exact. I had to figure out what the hell I was going to do. I stopped at a nearby bus stop and pulled out all the change I had in my pocket. I had about $20 and three dollars in change. I decided I would just get on the bus and ride it toward downtown. I had to clear my head, strategize my next move. I saw the Woodward coming and I boarded, taking a seat toward the back of the bus. I had so much going on. Life just seemed to get worse and worse for me. I couldn't use my cell to call Jasmyn or Desmond because the battery had died. While on the bus, I came to the realization that I was now a homeless teen. I stared out the window, trying to hold back my tears, so the passengers wouldn't catch the tears of sorrow and the misery falling from my face. But it was inevitable as they poured down like the rain outside. I just wanted to escape from the world I was in. I just wanted to, one day, wake up and be in another place. I closed my eyes and imagined I was surrounded by a family that truly had love and admiration for me.

I had drifted to sleep and, obviously, had been sleeping for far too long because, when I awoke, I was the only one on the bus at the Transit Depot. I had slept on the bus all night, and it was morning, and I knew I had to get off soon before a driver noticed me. I grabbed my luggage and struggled for a bit, but I pressed my body against the door, and it slid open. I walked around, hopeless and hungry. I stopped at a nearby coffee shop and had just enough to order a sandwich and an OJ. My stomach growled so loud that I just knew someone heard it. I hadn't eaten since yesterday afternoon, so, when my food came, I didn't waste any time devouring it. After paying for my meal, I tried to plan just what I would do and where I would lay my head down that night. The cold concrete was certainly not an option for me. I started to get a horrible stomach ache. I didn't know if it came from the food or my anxiety about my situation. I rushed to the bathroom and vomited immediately. I tried to stand, but the cramps I felt just had me weak in the knees. Eventually the pain subsided, and I returned to my table and had some saltines and water.

Later that day, I decided to stop by Jasmyn's house. Luckily, she didn't stay too far away from where I was at the coffee shop. I couldn't understand just what was going on with my body that kept making me feel so sick. I hoped maybe she could help me out.

"So how long have you been feeling this sick?" she questioned.

"Just this morning. I don't know what's going on with me," I responded.

"Well, what did you have for breakfast?"

"A sandwich and some OJ, but I threw that back up."

"Here. I got a few things for you—Tums, Pepto-Bismol, oh and a pregnancy test."

"A pregnancy test! What the hell you go and get a pregnancy test for? Ain't nobody pregnant?" I practically yelled at her.

"Danielle, just please take it. It may be the answer to why you feel so sick."

"Okay, whatever."

I snatched the First Response pregnancy test from Jasmyn and rolled my eyes as I muttered under my breath, "How dare she accuse me of being pregnant? What the hell is she on…drugs? There is certainly no way in hell I can be pregnant, so I'll take the test anyway just for kicks." I took the applicator out of the box and followed the directions. Supposedly, in five minutes, the fate of my life would forever be changed. If I was pregnant, which I knew I wasn't, what in the world would I do?

After the allotted time passed, I went to check the results from the test. I was in a world of surprise. There were two pink lines on my testing stick. This was a positive pregnancy test result. I took the test again with the second applicator just to make sure it wasn't a false positive, but there it was, the same results—pregnant, pregnant, and pregnant.

I grabbed the stick, left the room, and joined Jasmyn in the living room where she was watching *Good Morning, America* while sipping a Starbucks coffee she'd purchased earlier. She was so sophisticated. I knew deep down inside I truly admired her.

"So what did it say? Negative, right?" she questioned enthusiastically.

"Nope. I took the test twice. Both were positive. I'm pregnant. I'm going to be somebody's mom, and Desmond will be a dad." I felt tears sneak out of my eye ducts.

"It's okay, Danielle. It's not the end of the world. In the meantime, try taking these antacids for your nausea," she consoled as she passed me a bottle of Tums and a glass of water.

"Not the end of the world? I'm only sixteen. I have no place to stay. I'm basically homeless. What the hell am I going to do with a baby? I'm a baby myself."

"Well, we can start by telling Desmond that he's going to be a father."

"I know he won't be happy about this. No guy ever is."

"You don't know that. It's, at least, worth a try to let him know. Where is he right now?"

Jasmyn and I found Desmond hanging outside the school, watching a scrimmage between two high school football teams. I caught him posted by the gate while the game took place. I told Jasmyn she could go on ahead. I had to talk to Desmond alone. This mess I had found myself in was beyond serious.

"What is it, Danielle? What's going on with you?" he greeted me, kissing my forehead.

"I have to talk to you. It's serious. I don't need you backing out of this either."

"What's going on, D?" he asked, concerned.

"I just thought you ought to know that I'm pregnant."

"You're what?" he screamed out.

"Shh! Yes, I'm pregnant. We're going to be parents. I didn't have sex by myself. So don't you dare act like this baby isn't yours because you were the only guy I was with. Maybe you slept with a lot of girls, but...what are you going to do? So what? Are you going to try to claim this baby isn't yours?"

"Danielle, shut up! Let me talk. Damn. I didn't say I wasn't going to take care of the baby. I didn't say anything because you didn't give me a chance. I'm a little surprised. This is a lot to take in right now. But we both know what we did. We have to step up for the baby. I didn't say I was leaving. Besides, why would I leave now when you need me the most? Don't worry, Danielle. We'll figure out something. It'll be all right," he comforted me as he embraced me with a tight hug and a kiss on the lips.

Desmond was the rock in my life that I needed right now. He helped me to believe that, just maybe, things would be all right. I honestly had no idea what to do right now. It was always one thing after another. I mean, getting molested by my sadistic father, then learning that he wasn't actually my father, my mother not wanting me in her life, my aunt putting me out. Now, if things weren't bad enough, I was an abandoned and homeless pregnant teen.

Chapter 9

Living in Hell

Finding out that I was pregnant was the most terrifying thing that has happened to me. I was beyond scared. I had a baby growing inside of me with nowhere to live, no job, or any money. Sadly enough, I had no other options. I couldn't believe that I was doing this, but, since my aunt wouldn't allow me to move back in, I had to see if I could move back in with my mother. Did I want to? Hell no. Of course not. But where else could I go?

I walked up to the porch and stared at the house of hell where I'd been tortured for years. I swallowed my pride as I slowly approached the front door and prayed my father was not home. I was in no mood to see that sick bastard. I knocked on the door and waited for my mother to let me in. She must have not known it was me because she opened the door immediately.

"Look who's showed up at my doorstep. Why are you here? What do you want? Some money? I'm not giving you a damn thing," she stated.

"Mom, can I come in?" I requested.

"You're here, aren't you? Call me Cheryl, will you? Thank you."

"Look, I know I left, but I need a favor, Mom...I mean, Cheryl. I really need a place to stay, and I was wondering if I could stay here."

"You're joking, right? Why in the hell would I let you stay here again? It took me sixteen years just to get rid of your ass. Now you're trying to come back? Girl, you must be out of your damn mind. Why do you need to move back in here? What kind of trouble have you gotten yourself into now, lil girl?"

I hated how my mother constantly belittled me. She sat there at the kitchen table, smoking her cigarette without a care in the world about me or my pain.

"Hello! I said, what trouble have you gotten yourself into? You had to do something or else you wouldn't be here?"

"If you must know, I just found out I'm pregnant," I said sadly, knowing things would just get worse from here.

"Why does that not surprise me? I always knew your little hot ass wouldn't amount to shit in life. This just confirms it."

"Mom, I don't really need to hear all of your negativity right now. I just need somewhere to stay until I get on my feet."

"Well, sorry. I can't help you. Do you want me to feel sympathy for you because you went out and became a little ho and got knocked up? I am finally beginning to enjoy my life. I'm getting back the life your ungrateful ass stole from me?"

"That I stole from you?" I questioned.

I couldn't understand how a woman could be so bitter and cold toward her own child. This just didn't make any sense to me. *What the hell is wrong with this woman?*

"Yes, I just got my man back. Warrington is back. He is with me now. You tried to take him from me, but he is with me now."

"Mom, what are you talking about?"

"How the hell do you think I felt knowing the man that I love would rather fuck my own daughter than me? For three years, you were the backstabbing whore that stood in between me and him. He was my man, and you took him from me."

"What are you talking about? He was my father, and he raped me every day for three years. I begged for you to help me, but you never did. You let him torture me. You allowed him to take my innocence away," I cried to her.

"You deserved it. He took your innocence. You took my life from me. Ever since you came into my life, you have been nothing but trouble. You have taken every man I had from me."

"So, you allowed him to screw me just to keep him happy?"

"He's still here, isn't he?"

"Why didn't you just give me up for adoption if you hated me so much?" I questioned this woman with so much anger in her heart.

"And let you have a chance at a better life than me? Yeah right. I was raised in hell, and so would you... My mother was a cracked-out druggie who barely took care of me. I had to learn how to fend for my damn self out there in those streets. So when I got pregnant, my whole world came crumbling down. Your father didn't want you, so Warrington stepped in and did what needed to be done."

"My real father...?" I questioned as if I didn't know Warrington was not my father.

"Yes, your father Patrick Harris. He was a married man who didn't want word to get out that he'd impregnated some prostitute from the streets of Detroit because it would mess up his cushy life in the suburbs of Sterling Heights. He left me, and I never saw him again and it was your fault. You ruined everything," she said condescendingly.

"You got pregnant by one of the Johns you were paid to have sex with?"

I couldn't believe that my mother was revealing all of this information to me. My whole life was just a huge mistake, and no one wanted me. Cheryl was making this very obvious, but—Damn!—this was some crazy mess to take in.

"Yes, honey...you were the bastard child that nobody wanted. Oh, don't start crying on me now, Danielle. You'll see. That little kid of yours will make your life a living hell, just like you made mine. You're going to turn out to be just like me. Just you wait and see. You're sixteen with a baby and no job. How in the hell are you going to take care of a baby? What? Go get on welfare? Go get a job? Where you gonna stay? You ain't got shit going in your life, and, now with this child on the way, you never will. Life just happens like that."

"I will never be like you. I will never put my child through the selfish, cruel, and unimaginable things you've put me through. You are evil...just pure evil."

"I had to be. You took everything from me...everything. My freedom, my happiness, and my love. I hate you. Now I have the opportunity to get it all back."

"How can you stand here and say this to me? Haven't you ever loved me?"

"Danielle, love is for the weak at heart. The world preys on the weak. I am glad you are grown. I am glad you are gone. Now, I want you to get out of my house and out my life. Warrington is on his way home, and I don't need you here."

"So you don't even care to help your grandchild?"

"I have no grandchild because you are not my child. Now will you please leave?"

"I hate you!" I yelled to her before leaving.

"The feeling is mutual, my dear," I heard her faintly say as she walked away.

I couldn't believe this woman was so cold to me. She walked off toward her bedroom, and I just sat there for a moment and cried. This woman was a heartless bitch who only cared about herself. Since she didn't want me in her life, I swore I would never contact her again. I didn't need that energy around me when I was pregnant.

I gathered myself together and walked out of the house. As I walked down the street, I wiped tears of pain away from my face. I could see that the world had been mean to her, so she took her anger out on me. I didn't deserve this. No one deserved the shit I had been subjected to. Who in the hell would allow a man to screw her daughter just to keep the man in the house? Any woman who condoned this behavior needed to be put in prison. I promised myself that I would try to be a better mother to my child. But the truth was, I didn't know what the hell I would do now. I was still only sixteen years old, with no job, no money, and no place to stay with a child growing in my stomach.

The only other option I had left was to tell Desmond I needed a place to stay. He was the one who got me into this trouble in the first place. Clearly, he had to have a plan that could help us.

I was sitting at a neighborhood park waiting on Desmond to meet me. We had to discuss plans on what we would do between now and the next nine months. I glanced at a few kids playing just a couple of feet away from me on the slide. It just made me think of how I wanted a much better life for whoever was growing inside of me. The truth of the matter was, how could I? I had stopped going to school six months ago. So I was basically a dropout. What would I do now? Caught up in my own sorrow, I didn't even realize Desmond standing in front of me.

"So what's going on, Danielle? How are you feeling?" he questioned me.

"I need a place to stay, Des. I mean, we need a place to stay," I answered as I placed my hand on my stomach.

"Aren't you staying with family?"

"If I was, why would I have called you to come meet me? I have nowhere to stay. Where can I stay?"

"All right. I'll see if you can move in with me until we can get a place of our own."

"What the hell are we going to do for money?" I asked, frustrated.

"I'll just get a second job. I'm almost eighteen now. I'll take care of us. Don't worry, Danielle. Everything will be all right. You need to stop worrying. It's not healthy for the baby. I promise I will take care of us," he said, kissing me on the cheek and giving me a tight squeeze.

I wanted to believe him, but, because everyone had betrayed me in my life, I had a feeling he would soon be no different.

A Week Later

I had a strange nagging feeling at the bottom of my stomach as we pulled up to Desmond's mother's house.

He told me once before that the two of them weren't really close. Now, I would have the chance to find out just the reason for that.

"I hope you're ready for this," he said nervously, inhaling a deep breath as he opened the door.

I figured, if I could accept my mother not loving me and not wanting to be in my life, this couldn't be any worse. I would soon see.

We walked into the house and found his mother glued to the TV, watching an episode of *Judge Joe Brown*. She was medium height and stocky. She appeared to have a nasty attitude.

"Hey, Ma," Desmond greeted anxiously.

"Danielle, this is my mom. Mom, this is Danielle," Desmond said as he introduced us.

"Ooh, so this is the little tramp you got pregnant," she shouted out as her eyes shifted back and forth from the TV screen to me.

"Mama, don't be so rude to her, and I didn't just get her pregnant. She's my girlfriend."

"Dammit, boy, how many times have I told you about not bringing your trash home?"

"Ma, I really don't need you being rude to Danielle. Now I brought her by because you said you would allow her to stay here until we got on our feet."

"Why can't you stay at your parent's home?"

"I just can't. It's a complicated situation," I answered, not wanting to explain further.

"Well, you don't have any other family that you can stay with?"

"No, ma'am, I do not," I replied sadly.

"Um...well don't get too comfortable around here. Everybody who stays here has to earn their stay. But we'll talk about that tomorrow. Desmond take her to that extra bedroom down the hall. She can stay there," she ordered.

A Couple of Days Later

I came downstairs to make a sandwich, and, as I was looking in the fridge, I saw Desmond's mother looking over at me.

"Just what are you doing?" she questioned.

"I'm making a sandwich. I'm hungry."

"Who told you it was okay to eat up my food?"

"Well, what else am I supposed to eat?"

"I don't care, but I sure hope you don't think you are going to be staying here for free and eating up all the food in my house. Oh, no, un-uh not going to happen," she complained.

"What do you want me to do?"

"I suppose you could close my refrigerator and find yourself a job because you need to earn your stay. Your rent of $300 and another hundred for food will be due at the end of the month, and, if I don't get it, you gon' get out of my house. Do I make myself clear? I hope you weren't planning on staying here for free? Ain't a damn thing free in the real world."

"What...? You're making me pay rent? I've never paid rent a day in my life. How am I supposed to pay rent? I don't have a job. I don't even know how to get a job," I cried out in shock.

"That is not my problem, sweetheart. Perhaps you and my son should have thought of that before you tried to be so damn grown. I suggest you find a job, or use what got you pregnant in the first place," she said, walking away.

I couldn't believe this woman was making an unemployed, pregnant teen pay her almost $400 a month. That was a lot of money. *What the hell would I do to get that?* I didn't know what to do because there was nothing else left for me. This was my last resort. I just hoped Desmond would help me out through all this madness. I walked to his room to see if I could understand why his mother would want to do this to us when we were already struggling. I knocked on his door and found him lacing up some Jordans on his feet. I went to sit on the bed and began to cry a little.

"What's wrong, Danielle?"

"Your mother just told me that I had to pay her $400. I don't have that kind of money. Doesn't she know about our situation? That's why we're here in the first place."

"Oh, yeah. About that, she's making me pay her $200 just to kick it here."

"What...? Why the hell am I paying her two hundred dollars more than you? You need to talk to her about that. That isn't fair. You're the one with the job."

"I'll talk to her. Don't sweat it. She's just tripping."

Just as he said that, his mother happened to pop in the room to see what we're doing.

"Who's tripping? What are y'all talking about?"

"We were minding our own business, before you got so nosy," I muttered underneath my breath.

"What? Excuse me, little girl? Did you say something? Because if you have something to say, you can say it nice and loud."

I rolled my eyes and stared at Desmond to defend me, but he did nothing but stare at his stupid shoes.

"Yes, I do have something to say. I want to know why I have to pay four and he pays two."

"Because, I don't appreciate my son bringing home little sluts like you to ruin his life."

I elbowed Desmond and gave him a mean glare. Apparently, he could tell I was angry because he finally stopped messing with his shoes and looked up. "Mom, we're just saying, we don't think it's fair. That's all. And you could be a little nicer to Danielle."

"Excuse me? What did you say, you little piece of shit? Are you defending this girl in my house? I make the rules in this house. I pay the bills in the house. I run shit in this house. I do what I damn well please in my house. If you don't like it, you can move. But you can't because you have nowhere to go because you fucked some trick and got her pregnant. Now you need mother to help you out with a place to stay. You little ingrate, you should be glad I let you and your little girlfriend live in my house, yet you want to complain because you can't stay rent free. Well, too damn bad. Life ain't fair. Get over it," his mother ranted.

She turned and walked away. I just saw Desmond lower his head down as if he was embarrassed. I could see staying here was not a good idea either. I had to make some changes, and I had to make them quick, but, with no job, it would be hard.

With each turning day, Desmond's mother, Aretha, would have me living in straight hell. I couldn't do anything in her house without her complaining about something. It was really as if she was the devil's sister.

Every day was a constant reminder of how I owed her money and how I should be thankful that she took me in as I had nothing and was going nowhere fast in life. I needed money, and I needed cash fast. It wasn't going to be easy making this dough, but I had to make moves, and they had to be done now, and I knew just what I would do sadly enough.

Chapter 10

The Hate I Felt Inside

I hated this fucking baby growing inside me. I wished it would die. It was already making my life miserable. I was mad that I didn't have money or insurance for an abortion. I hoped for a miscarriage, but that day never came. *What will I do with a baby? There is no way in hell I can be someone's mother. I don't even want this damn thing.* Desmond could raise it by himself for all I cared. My life was already fucked up, and I didn't need anything or anyone else adding to it. Plus, I didn't want to mess this child's life up. Naw, no one needed to endure the pain and misery I grew up dealing with.

I stood outside the house on the porch just contemplating what to do next. I had to find ways to come up with some money. I had told Desmond numerous times to get us the hell out of his mother's house. But still he did nothing. Two months had come and gone since I'd started living there. I hated it. His mother was a complete bitch all of the time. I believe the only thing she helped me with was going to apply for welfare. That shit was barely enough to make ends meet. I needed real money, and I needed it now. I had to get away from this nightmare that I was living in once and for all.

I heard the screen door open as I continued standing on the porch, looking at the neighborhood. It was Desmond, coming out to talk to me…yet again.

"Danielle, what the hell are you doing smoking a damn cigarette when you're three months pregnant?" he asked frustrated.

"I'm stressed out, Desmond. I told you that I didn't want this damn baby. You won't believe me."

"Oh, D, you don't mean that. We're just having a rough time right now." He tried to convince me of some shit that I had already made up in my mind.

"What do you mean it's not what I mean? What the hell are we going to do with a damn baby, Desmond? We don't even have our own place. I've told you over and over again to get us the hell out of your mom's place. That woman hates me. She is so damn evil. You don't even stand up to her. She even treats you like shit, and you don't do a damn thing about it. I'm sick of living here," I yelled as we continued to argue back and forth.

"Well, what the hell do you suppose that I do? I'm trying to please you and my damn mother. I'm saving money, so we can get our own spot. Things just take time, Danielle. That's all. I know you want to leave. I do, too, but come on. Just give me some time. I just got a second job downtown. All I ask is—"

"I know to give you time and be patient," I said as I rolled my eyes and walked off the porch.

"Where are you going? It's starting to get late, Danielle."

"To go make some money," I said as I began walking down the street.

That was all Desmond could tell me—to be patient. I was working on it, but I couldn't put up with too much more of this shit. I had to take matters into my own hands, and I had to do it soon.

I walked to the nearby pawn shop to get some cash for the jewelry I had stolen from my mother before I left my parents' house. I had taken a gold necklace, two diamond rings, and a tennis bracelet. My mother didn't deserve nice shit. She wasn't a nice person. I'm sure she wouldn't miss any of those things. Warrington could just buy her more, right? The clerk in the store gave me $300 for this stuff. It wasn't as much as I wanted, but fuck it. I still needed the money, something about some shit depreciating in value or whatever. I just took the cash and walked out the store. As I made my way down the block, I was stopped by this guy who looked like a

Hollywood rapper. I had to admit. He was a caramel cutie, real easy on the eyes with a nice smile.

"Hello, beautiful, where are you going in such a rush?" he questioned.

"Um, I guess I'm going home," I answered.

"So soon? I didn't even get a chance to kick it with you yet."

"I don't even know you," I replied nervously.

"Honey, my name is Dante Harris, and I want to spend the night with you. Can we make this happen?" he requested, kissing my hand.

"You're a little forward, aren't you?"

"Yeah, yeah, what's your name?"

"Danielle, Danielle Turner," I answered shyly.

"All right, Danielle Turner, can we spend the night together?"

"We don't know one another," I said as I tried to brush past him, but he just wouldn't let me go.

"I'm serious. I'm willing to pay you $400 to kick it with me," Dante said to me with a huge grin on his face.

"What? You think I'm a prostitute?"

"No, I'm just interested in spending time with a beautiful woman. I'm sure you need the cash. I'm good for it. Danielle. I can make the night worth your while."

I knew I shouldn't have even considered it, but, if this dude was truly willing to pay me cold, hard cash just to kic it with him, I would be a fool to turn it down.

"Okay, what you are trying to do?"

"Anything you want, pretty lady. I won't hurt you. I promise. My place is right down the street."

He pointed to a luxury car parked five feet away from where we were standing. I figured, with everything I'd been through in my life, things couldn't get any worse. I got inside his 2014 Lincoln MKS and prayed he wasn't a crazed rapist as he drove me to his house on Fenkell and Wyoming. It was a decent neighborhood for this part of town. He parked the car and opened the passenger side door.

"We're here, sweetness."

I stood there frozen as he tried to lead up the stairs to the front door.

"Come on now, Danielle. I told you everything would be all right. We are already here, so you might as well come on in."

He had a point. I was on the far west side of town. Way too damn far to walk home toward Gratiot. We finally went inside Dante's house, and it was as if he had won the lottery or something. Dude was loaded. He had two HD plasma TVs hanging up in almost every room and a white Persian rug that matched the white leather furniture set in the living room. I had never seen anything like this. I had to know how he had acquired this much money, so I could get a part of this. He led me to the bedroom, which was swallowed by a California King size bed with red satin sheets and matching bed-spread. I sat at the edge of the bed because I was too afraid of wrinkling any of his sheets. I watched him as he took his Cartier glasses off and laid them on the dresser. He removed his jacket, and I could tell by his arms and his chest that he worked out.

"So where did you get all that expensive stuff from?" I questioned, concerned that he might be a drug dealer.

"I'm in the adult entertainment business. I make big money. I run Club Coliseum. You don't know about me? You must not be from the D then?" he boasted.

"No, I'm from Detroit, but I've just never heard of the club."

"Well, trust me, I can take care of you, to the point where you'll never have to work again. I can have you walking away with two or four thousand dollars a night. All you have to do is work for me. I promise you, Danielle. I can give you the world."

He took a seat next to me on the bed. I had to admit. He was sexy as hell. He gazed into my eyes as he softly kissed my back then my lips and began to undress me. I knew that what I was doing wasn't right, but I couldn't turn down extra money. This was my ticket. Dante had come right on time. He was a man with both money and power, and these two key things could change my life forever.

The next day, Dante and I got dressed after a night of pleasurable sex. My mouth dropped open as he reached into his wallet and handed me four crisp one hundred dollar bills. I couldn't believe he had made it so easy for me to make this money. I went from being broke to having $700 that night. The combination of sex and money was too powerful to resist. I had to come back for more.

Later that day, Dante dropped me off back home, and, just as I had guessed it, there was Desmond sitting right there on the porch as I got out of the car. He had a disgusted look on his face which grew as Dante kissed me on the cheek before he drove off down the street. I walked up to the porch to go inside, knowing he was going to make a scene first.

"Can you explain to me what the mother of my child is doing getting out of another man's car?"

"Oh my goodness, Desmond, that was nothing. He was just a friend."

"Friend my ass. You've been gone all damn night. I was waiting up for you. What the fuck you been doing out all…"

He stopped himself mid-sentence and looked at me as if he was going to hit me.

I might have been frustrated with him, but I was no fool. I was three months pregnant, and Desmond was over six feet tall. I ducked out of the way to miss his swing at me.

"I'm not going to hit you, Danielle...but just tell me one thing. Did you fuck this dude? Tell me the truth. I see dude dropping you off in an expensive-ass car, kissing on you and shit. You cheating on me, bitch? Here I am, busting my ass, working two jobs, so I can get a house for our family, and you sneaking around on me? Please tell me you didn't have sex with that dude. If you did, get your stuff and get the hell out of my house. You couldn't even stop to, at least, think of the baby we're about to have."

"I didn't do anything, Desmond, but find a way to make myself some money. Now if you'll excuse me. I'm...I mean, we're really tired. I'm going in the house to lie down," I said, walking past him and making my way inside the house.

I felt bad for Desmond. I knew I shouldn't have lied. He didn't deserve that, but I had learned to look out for numero uno. I cared for Desmond wholeheartedly, but I had also witnessed the same people who claimed to love me turn around and hurt me. There was no way of telling if he would be any different. What I did know was that I would certainly have to contact Dante again for another fix.

Chapter 11

Surprises

Another night out with Dante at Iridescence, one of the most expensive restaurants in Detroit, had me feeling like I was the most important woman in his life. Truthfully, we'd only known each other for a short period of time, but the chemistry was amazing. The two of us were discussing the scenery at the restaurant when a waiter sat a beautiful bouquet of roses on our table. I didn't know where they came from or why they were there until he picked up the card and read it to me:

To the most beautiful girl in the world, words can't express how much you mean to me. I know it hasn't been long since we've known each other, but to me it's been forever.

That was the sweetest thing anyone had ever done for me. Dante was like a gift sent from heaven. He satisfied all of my needs and desires. I never had to worry about money ever again because he provided it for me. He had given me a sense of security when all my hope was lost.

The more time I spent with him, the more I forgot all about Desmond. But there was actually no way I could forget I was carrying his baby. I wanted things to progress with us, but I knew, at this moment, it was out of the question.

"Thank you, Dante. That was absolutely beautiful. I have never had anyone give me flowers before. You are very sweet."

"That brings me to my question. What do you think about moving in with me? I mean, if things are going so well between us, we should move to the next step, right?" he questioned me while cutting into his grilled chicken.

I didn't know how to answer that. I wanted things to go further, but I knew it just wouldn't be right.

"I don't think I can do that. I'm kind of involved with someone, and we're soon to be parents. But things between us aren't going well. I'm just staying around because I have nowhere else to go. He's kind of…well, his mother is providing me with a roof over my head, although I hate being there."

"Well, it doesn't seem like you're too happy to me, but if that's where you want to be…"

"Oh, no, of course not. I just don't have anywhere else to go right now, and living there is where I'm at right now."

"Well, you know I have a place that I sure wouldn't mind you living in. I really care about you, Danielle. I keep telling you that I can take care of you if only you'd let me. I wish you would listen."

"Things just aren't that easy…"

"You're just afraid. Just trust me, please. I wish you would give me a chance."

I understand that he wanted to give me the life I'd never had before, but what would I tell Desmond. *What about the baby we were having?* I didn't know what to do. I just knew that there was a part of me that wanted to be with Dante. I couldn't let him go. I was hooked, and he was my true addiction. He had already given me $400 before we came out to the restaurant. I just couldn't imagine that he was truly making enough cash to continue paying me like this.

After our dinner date, we headed back to his place. It was late, almost one in the morning. I checked my phone while Dante was in the bathroom and saw that I had seven missed calls from Desmond and five text messages asking where the hell I was. I didn't answer because I felt like I didn't have to.

I wasn't his child. I turned my phone off and forgot all about his failed attempts to contact me. I got weak when I saw Dante coming out the bathroom with just his boxers on. He was my sexual chocolate that I couldn't get enough of. He walked over to me, pushed me down on the bed, and ran his hands up my thighs until he reached my panties. He slowly pulled my panties down, then whispered in my ear how much he loved me. There was no holding back. I could feel myself squirming as he entered me. I grabbed on to him tightly, scratching his back while moaning as his manhood stroked the moist walls inside of me. The vibration of his penis penetrating inside of me had me screaming. This was not supposed to be an emotional attachment. It was supposed to be just for profit. I was supposed to satisfy him in the bed, and he was supposed to satisfy my wallet with a few new Benjamins. But the more time I spent alone with him, the more I couldn't help but get attached. He complemented me in so many ways.

***

The next morning, I woke up with a note taped to my wallet and a box of jewelry on the nightstand while he was freshening up in the shower. The note read:

Look inside. I have a surprise for you.

I opened my wallet to see ten one-hundred dollar bills. My mouth dropped open. I couldn't believe he had placed a thousand dollars in my wallet. He had already given me four hundred dollars earlier. This was just amazing to me. The jewelry box was so beautiful. It was a gold square box with a royal blue bow tied around it. I opened the box and found a diamond tennis bracelet inside. I cried little tears of joy that just poured out of me. This just made me so happy. I ran into the bathroom to see Dante shaving. I gave him the biggest hug in the world.

"I see that you got the stuff I left you," he said in between stroking the razor against his smooth face.

"Yes, I did, and I just want to say thank you. I love it. I love you, honey. Oh, my goodness. This bracelet is beautiful."

"I'm glad that you like it. I was really thinking that you should re-think your decision about moving in with me. I know you have things that you have to deal with, but I thought, in six months after the birth of your baby, you could move in with me. You don't have to answer now. Just think about it," he said, looking down at my stomach.

It was a lot to think about. I didn't want to hurt Desmond. He had taken me in when there was no one else there for me. And this was how I was repaying him. But at the same time, I'd told him numerously to get us out of his mother's home. Months had gone by, and we were still living there. I was tired of it. I needed a change, and Dante was becoming the change that I needed.

****

I made my way back to Desmond's place later that day at around five p.m. I knew things would be heated between us once I walked through the door. But I took it like a grown woman and dealt with whatever he wanted to rant about. I walked to my room and saw him sitting on my bed with an angry look on his face.

"Close the damn door!" he yelled at me.

"What's wrong now, Desmond?" I questioned annoyingly.

"Where the hell were you for the past couple days? I was trying to reach you like crazy. You're lucky my mother didn't change the locks."

"That's just it. Here we go again. Two damn parents living in another parent's house. Aren't you tired of this? I sure as hell know I am."

"Oh, shit! Here we go. We on this again, Danielle. So you'd rather be running around on me, then trying to work shit out with me? I'm the father of your child. Danielle. Or did you forget that you were still pregnant? What the hell is that on your arm?" he questioned, referring to the bracelet on my left arm. I had forgotten to take it off before I walked into the house.

"It's nothing, Desmond, just a bracelet," I said, waving it off.

"Who gave it to you? Was it that same dude?"

I rolled my eyes and pointed toward the door to give him a hint to get out of my room.

"I'm really tired, Desmond. Can we talk about this tomorrow?"

"You're a selfish-ass bitch, Danielle, really. Moms and I took you in when nobody else wanted your trifling ass, and this is how you repay us? Damn! I should've known you was a hood rat."

"What the hell did you just call me? Did you just call me a fucking hood rat? You don't know a damn thing about me, Desmond. You don't! You want to know why I couldn't stay with my own family? I'll tell you. Let me school you on my life before I met you! When I was thirteen years old, my father was a drunk who used to come into my room and fuck me. Yes, I said it, Desmond. My father molested me for about three years until I decided to run away. Then, I tried to stay with my aunt and then she put me out. And do you want to know what my mother did about me being molested? Nothing! She didn't do a damn thing! She stood there and watched as my father molested me. She told me to be quiet and take it right before she left the room. My parents never gave a damn about me! When I asked if I could move back in, once I found out I was pregnant, she humiliated me. She told me that my father who had molested me for years was never my real father, but some drunk she stayed with for her own personal gain. My real father was a John she got paid to have sex with. My life was crap, and our baby will be crap. I told you I didn't want this baby. I just wanted someone to love me. That's all I wanted, that's all I wanted..."

I fell to my knees in tears as I confessed my painful secrets to Desmond. He rushed over to me with tears in his eyes. He comforted me with a tight squeeze and a kiss on the forehead. At that moment, I knew that I could count on him, too. I was confused. I didn't want to lose neither one of these guys. They both were good for me, but for two different reasons. I needed Desmond for the emotional connection. Plus, he was the father of my child. We had to be a part of each other's lives for the next eighteen years regardless, but Dante satisfied me with money which I needed badly. But I knew I had to get myself together before the birth of this baby or I'd be more screwed up than I already was.

Chapter 12

Labor & Pain

Six months later, I gave birth to a beautiful, six-pound baby girl who I named Kylie Monique Turner. She had a head full of hair and came out looking just like me and Desmond. Giving birth was the most excruciating pain I had ever felt. I looked my baby in her eyes and thought, She's just like me. Hell. She is me reincarnated. I wanted to give her the best life possible. If only things were that easy. Me and Desmond were still living at his mother's house, although he claimed there was almost enough money for us to get ourselves a one-bedroom apartment. I was still seeing Dante behind Desmond's back. Desmond didn't know that Dante was the money ticket that had helped me rack up around three to four thousand dollars. I was just looking for a way to escape. A way to leave him and start a new life with Dante. I knew being with him would be the right way to go. He would provide me with enough money to take care of Kylie. Desmond was a good person, but good people don't pay bills and raise babies, money does.

We had been home with our baby girl Kylie for two weeks now. I loved that baby with everything in me, but I just couldn't take it anymore. She was a newborn that cried all of the time. I never got any damn sleep because I was up with her all of the time while Desmond went to work and school. His mother never watched her grand-daughter. She just constantly complained about her crying. I needed a break. I was growing tired of always being the one stuck with her. I needed to see Dante because my funds were getting low. I had spent all I had on shit for this crybaby I just popped out.

Desmond's mother had left for work about an hour ago, and he would be leaving soon too. Another damn night of me being stuck alone with her. This wasn't fair. I wanted to be free, free from hearing her cries, free from having to change stinky-ass diapers. Free from being a mother and all of its responsibilities. I was in our bedroom where I just finished feeding her when Desmond told me he was leaving for work early.

"My boss called me in a little early, and, since we're trying to move, we can really use the money. Are you going to be all right with Kylie tonight?"

"Dammit, Desmond! Why are you always leaving me alone with this baby? I have a life, too, you know?"

"I know that, Danielle, but, right now, you are the only one that can watch the baby. She just ate. She's just going to fall asleep for a couple hours. Where else do you have to go? Stop complaining, and take care of the baby. I'm going to work," he said as he grabbed his valet jacket and walked out the door.

I let out a loud cry as he closed the door behind himself. I put the baby down in her crib and sat on the bed. I stared at Kylie and wondered if this was what my life would be like from now on. Me, just sitting at home with a crying baby. Suddenly, my phone rang. I picked it up and answered immediately once I realized who it was.

"Yo, Danielle, long time no hear from. What's been up? Can you come out tonight? I really need to see you." Dante told me cheerfully.

"Um, yeah, it has been a while, Dante. I've really missed you."

"I've missed you, too, hun. Can you get out tonight?"

"Um...sure. I can get out," I replied confused as I stared at baby Kylie sleeping peacefully. "Yes, I can come out tonight."

"Cool. I'll come get you in about an hour," he assured me before he hung up the phone.

That was exactly the boost I needed to lift my spirits up. I did need to get out of the house. I had grown so tired of always being the one left with this baby. Now I had a chance to go out and do something. I was sure the baby would be fine. Newborns sleep for hours anyway, so, by the time, I came back to the house, I was sure she would still be asleep.

Dante came by to pick me up, and we went back to his house. I had always enjoyed our nights together. I had almost forgotten how sexy Dante was, and how good he made me feel. He was my drug, and I was truly hooked.

When we made it back to his house, he pulled me to the side and kissed me passionately. It was like we were in a different world that was made just for the two of us.

"I missed you, Danielle. I haven't seen you in so long."

"I missed you, too, Dante. Ugh, I've been feeling so trapped lately. I'm so glad you called. I can finally get a break and just have a life again."

"Why don't you have a drink with me? You know, to take your mind off of things. I told you that you needed to move in with me. I can take care of you and make you happy. Think about that, will you, Danielle?"

He poured me a glass of Peach Ciroc which tasted so sweet, I drank the whole bottle. We started taking shots of Patron and vodka. Over and over again, Dante and I shared such a good time together. I could feel myself getting a little tipsy. As I walked toward his bedroom, I almost tripped over the end table. We burst out laughing, as it was becoming apparent that I was obviously drunk. Again, Dante paid me $300 for my services again. It was cash I needed. As I slowly started to sober up, I realized that it was twelve-thirty in the morning. I had been over at Dante's for almost four hours now. This was way longer than I had intended. I had completely forgotten about Kylie. I prayed she was still sleep. I couldn't believe that I had left her in the house alone for that long. *What the hell is going on in my head?*

Dante dropped me off in front of the house, and I ran up the stairs to the porch and could hear the faint cry from Kylie in the house. I began panicking instantly. I searched my purse for the house keys but could not retrieve them. I knew I had to have my house keys, but I couldn't find them in my purse or my pocket. I started to hear Kylie's crying becoming louder and more forceful. I had been standing outside searching for a key or a way to open the door for about fifteen minutes now. The only thing I could think of was calling Desmond to have him come home early from his shift before his evil-ass mother came home and found out. There was just no way I could believe that I had locked my baby in the house. What the hell was I thinking? I pulled out my cell and dialed

Desmond's number. Luckily, he was on break and could answer the phone.

"What's up, Danielle? How's Kylie?" he questioned.

"Um…I kind of locked her inside the house. I thought I had my keys, but I didn't, and I was only going out for an hour and she was sleeping—"

"What the fuck do you mean you locked our baby in the house and you were only leaving for an hour? You are the mother. When you leave, you take the baby with you. Where are you?"

"I'm at the house. I just don't have my key to get in the house."

"What the hell? Danielle, anything could've happened to her. So you can't get inside the damn house…I'll be there in twenty minutes. Dammit! Girl, what the hell is wrong with you?" he yelled at me before hanging up in my ear.

I knew this looked bad. I was beginning to realize that I was becoming my mother. Her mother didn't want her; she didn't want me, and I didn't want mine. But I had told Desmond months ago, before Kylie was even born, that I wasn't ready to be a mother. Why he didn't pay for a damn abortion is beyond me. I pulled out a cigarette and lit it as I awaited Desmond's arrival. *I'm not in the mood for no damn lecture. He always feels the need to give me a damn lecture like he is my damn father. I don't have time for his bitter opinion.*

Sadly, to my dismay, Desmond not only showed up but so did his mother. I heard her cussing and rambling on about how she was going to kill me. This told me that he must have told her what happened. *Great! This is just what I need – a confrontation with his evil-ass mother.*

"Where she at? This is ridiculous. How the hell do you lock the baby in the house? She should've never left the house. Move, Danielle. Let me open the damn door," Aretha said in an aggravated tone.

I stood aside as she opened the door, and Desmond brushed past me to see why Kylie was crying. I followed him into the room, and he looked as if he was going to kill me.

"Danielle! She pissed everywhere. She needs her diaper changed, and she's probably hungry. Damn! I can't believe you left the baby alone for an hour."

"Um, it was more like a few hours, but I was trying to come right back, but I lost track of time."

"What the hell were you doing for just a few hours that you didn't think of your baby girl?"

"I had to go make some money…"

"Now, what I want to know is how the hell did you lock the baby in the house by herself? That's just irres-ponsible. Desmond, I'm going to see that you get full custody of this baby. I can tell you don't want this baby, do you, Danielle? I'm tired of you causing problems in my house. Now, Desmond, the baby can stay, but, Danielle, I can't have you living in my house anymore. You've got to go."

"Excuse me, but this is my baby, too," I reminded Aretha.

"I'm not gon' have you keep putting this baby life at risk, so you can pack your stuff up and find somewhere else to go," she said as she left the room.

"So what, Desmond? You agree with her?"

"Damn, Danielle. What do you think? You left our newborn baby in the house alone. Anything could've happened. This is Detroit. What if someone had broken in and kidnapped her or the house caught fire. I just can't risk that. You can still see her, but right now I don't know about having you stay alone with the baby."

"You know what? Forget you, Desmond. You never did stand up for me against your mother. You always acted like a punk bitch. Fine, you want me out. I'll go first thing in the morning. I've told you numerous times to get us a place for us, but still you haven't. I told you, before I had Kylie, that I wasn't ready to be a mother. I begged you for an abortion, but you said no, that we could get through this together."

"That's not a damn excuse, Danielle. Stop using that shit as an excuse. You fucked up. Now woman up and accept it. You put our baby in harm's way, and now you're trying to blame everybody but yourself."

"You know what? I don't need this. You want me out of here? Fine! I already got a man who can satisfy all of my needs. He actually makes money to take care of me. I just wasted my time being with you. You wanted the baby, Desmond. Now you got the baby. I'm done with this, and I'm done with you," I told him as I left his room where the baby was sleeping and walked down to my room.

I started packing my bags, so I could be out of there by the morning. I finally had found the escape I needed. I'd wanted to leave Desmond and his mother for some time now. Maybe, I subconsciously planned this, so I would have a way out. So I could have a reason to leave Desmond. He never defended me in front of his mother. He never did anything for me. I was free to now be with Dante, the one who could take care of me and provide for me the way I should be provided for. Besides, he'd been asking me to move in with him for the longest anyway. Now, we could finally be together. I knew things would start looking better for me.

Chapter 13

Dante's Prison

I felt like a weight had been lifted off my shoulders once I moved in with Dante. He was glad I finally accepted his offer and wondered why it took me so long. I was so relieved that I didn't have to worry any longer about the constant stress or misery that I felt while staying at Desmond's house. Everything in me knew things would be perfect from here on out. Later that evening, Dante prepared dinner for us on my first night of officially living with him. Things were so romantic. We ate our food by the candlelight and just talked. I haven't felt this happy in…I can't remember when I'd ever felt this good.

"You know, Danielle, I'm glad you finally decided to move in with me. I can really take care of you the way you need to be. Beautiful women always have such a soft spot in my heart," he said as he gently touched my face.

I reached out and grabbed his hand, a certain sense of warmth swept over me that slowly built up a security with him. I confessed to him the dark secret that I'd lived with all of my life. I knew he would be the one that could take away all of the pain and agony that plagued my heart every day.

"I'm only seventeen, but I've been through so much hell in my life. When I was just thirteen years old, my father raped me almost every day for three years until I decided to run away. My mother didn't do a damn thing. She allowed it to happen just to keep him satisfied. I tried staying with other people in my family, but I was just going from place to place, trying to find where I belong in this world. Now I got a little baby girl, and, as gorgeous as she is, I can't take care of her like she needs me to. I'm just not ready to be anybody's mother. I don't even know who the hell I am yet," I confessed as I played with my salmon and rice dinner.

"Wow, that's a lot to take in. I'm sorry you had to grow up like that. That's really fucked up, Danielle. I feel sorry for you. You need somebody in your corner that you can depend on. It seems as if everybody in your life has let you down. I just want to let you know that I am glad you are here with me. I want to be that person that will always be there for you. Danielle, I want to show you the other side of life. The finer things in life. You need to know that life isn't all about heartache and pain. There are things out there that can make you happy.

There are people out here that can make you smile. Let me be the one that makes you smile, makes you happy, just shows you that there are good people out here in this world," he said, giving me a sensual kiss on the lips.

I let a few tears fall from my eyes as he reassured me that he would take care of me. He took me by the hand and led me to the bedroom. Gently, he kissed my neck, as he laid me down on the bed and began to undress me slowly. I couldn't help but return the gesture. He looked so sexy to me as he stripped down to his boxers. I ran my fingers from his chest down to his tight six pack and pulled him close to me. I screamed as he entered me. The time we spent together was better than all the others. I moaned passionately as he stroked strongly inside of me. I couldn't help but let him know how good he was making me feel. There was truly something addictive about Dante, and I loved it. I fell in love with sex because of him. Hell! I was beginning to fall in love with him. He was taking away all of my frustrations that had been going on in my life. The best part of my life was when I would spend time with him.

****

At this point, I had been living with Dante for two weeks. I was sitting on the couch watching an old episode of a

BET TV show, as Dante walked in. He didn't appear to be in the best of moods, just by the frustration on his face. I was afraid to ask what was bothering him, but I proceeded anyway.

"Hey! What's going on, Dante? Why do you look so upset?"

"Danielle, when the hell are you going to go out and start making me my money? You been up in my house for almost three weeks now and you haven't made me any money. So now, I'm going to need you to get your ass outside and make my money," he demanded.

"Excuse me? What are you talking about 'make you your money'? I'm not a prostitute."

"What? You're not a what? Why the hell do you think I was paying you? It wasn't just because I found you attractive. Come on, girl. Did you really think that you were that special? You didn't even know me and you slept with me on the same night. That doesn't make you a ho? Girl, please. Now I'm going to need you to go out on those streets and work for me. And if you don't make, at least, three to four hundred dollars a night, you might as well not even come home. I'm serious, Danielle. You didn't think you were going to stay here for free, did you?"

"What the hell are you talking about, Dante? I'm not your damn prostitute. I'm not about to go sell my body just to give you money. That doesn't make…"

He cut me off with a hard slap across the face. I held my hand up to the side of my face. I was in shock. I couldn't believe how quickly his personality had changed on me.

"Bitch, what did I just tell you? I'm a businessman. The only thing that matters to me is money. And this is how I make mine. If it means pimpin' your ass out, so be it. I told you I worked for a club. I run those women. Now I run you."

"Dante, you must be out of your damn mind. I'm not having sex with random men, just to keep your pockets fat."

I couldn't believe what he was talking about. I got up from the couch and walked toward the bedroom until he pulled my arm and grabbed me tightly by the neck.

"You're going to do whatever the hell I tell you to, or you'll be finding your ass without a damn place to live. You know, right now you don't have anywhere else to fucking go. Nobody wants your ass. You been screwed and fucked over by some man you thought was your daddy. You ain't got no future. Where else you gon' go? Who else is going to take care of you? That's right.

Nobody, no damn body, but me. I've been taking care of you since day one."

"What the hell is wrong with you, Dante? Why are you changing up on me all of a sudden?"

"Ain't nobody changing up on you. This is the real me. I suggest you spend less time talking and more time figuring out how you plan on making my money tonight, or you will find yourself sleeping on those streets," he ordered before he slammed the bedroom door in my face.

I couldn't understand exactly what the hell was going on with him, but something told me there was no sense in testing him. I didn't want to go ahead with what he told me, but the sad truth was, I had nowhere else to go. What else was I supposed to do? *Damn, this is insane. I thought Dante would be my escape from all the bullshit that has repeatedly happened in my life. Everywhere I turn, I'm let down by some person in my life.*

As night fell, I found myself on the corner of Woodward along with some drugged out hookers. I couldn't believe this was my life. *How did I go from staying at my aunt's house to working on the streets for Dante? I was a fool for ever meeting him in the first place. I should've known he never really cared for me. I'm not even eighteen yet, and I've been through so much — raped, abandoned, teen mother, and now, becoming a prostitute. Damn! Where the hell is God? Why couldn't He save me from this damnation?*

I stood against a building as I watched the other women solicit men and drove away in their vehicles. A guy driving a red Expedition blew his horn at me. I tried to ignore it, but then I remembered what Dante said to me earlier. I walked up to the truck to see what he wanted.

"Hey there, pretty lady. What are you doing tonight? You thinking you may want to roll with me? Have a little fun? I'll make it worth your while. How does a hundred bucks sound?"

"What do you want?" I questioned nervously. I just wanted this night to be over with.

"Nothing special. Just a little sex, little bit of head. I got the money ready right here for you," he boasted, flashing crispy twenties in front of me.

He was an older guy. I'd say around his late twenties, but he wasn't bad looking. He appeared to have lots of money. I assumed he may have been a drug dealer with all the jewelry that hung around his neck. I needed the cash, so I got inside his truck and sat back as he drove us to a vacant lot downtown. This was the most degrading moment of my life, but I did what needed to be done. I imagined I was somewhere else, while this guy, who called himself Jose, had sex with me in the back seat of his truck. I couldn't lie. I felt like a slut for a minute. But the sex wasn't horrible. In fact, I enjoyed it, and fortunately protection was used. Sex was a way for me to feel satisfied, to forget my troubles, and find some peace within myself. Things still couldn't end soon enough in this situation though. He paid me after my services had been performed and drove me back to 7 Mile and Woodward.

The more I did this, the more comfortable I became. I worked with a few different guys that evening and made around three hundred and forty dollars. Man, if this was how much I could make in one night just for sleeping with a few guys, I could make twice this much if I did this regularly. Fuck feeling degraded, it was easy money, and there was never anything wrong with making some easy money. Plus, me and Dante split the money. He was happy I was bringing home the cash, and I was glad that I could keep my man.

After a couple weeks of being out on the streets, I became a regular enough to where the other ladies knew me, but still cool enough to keep a low profile from the cops. It didn't bother me because I stopped looking at the men as strangers I was sleeping with. Instead I looked at them as ATMS, ready and willing to give me whatever it was that I wanted. Money, money, money was all I wanted. It was all that mattered. Men took sex from me unwillingly, so hell now I could get paid to give them what it is they wanted. I soon learned that all that glitters ain't gold, and easy money ain't always the best money.

Chapter 14

Losing My Way

I was coming home or better yet heading to Dante's house after another exhausting night of making money. This time, I made $500.00. I walked through the door, and what did I see? Another damn woman sitting on his lap. I rushed over to them, and I pulled the girl off him. Dante had the nerve to push me out of the way.

"What the hell are you doing, Dante? Who is this? Are you messing with her?" I questioned him furiously.

"Danielle, don't worry about who she is. It's not important to you. Nothing happened between us. Why are you jumping to conclusions?"

He tried to cover up his mess with some lies to try and make me look stupid. I was trying to piece together exactly what was going on as he walked the female to the door. But her reaction startled me.

"Don't get comfortable here. You won't be here for too long," she said before walking out the door.

I didn't understand what she meant by her statement, but I did want to know why Dante had her in our house in the first place. I walked over to him as he rolled his eyes at me and began walking away.

"No, where are you going? I want to know who that woman was you had in our house?" I asked sternly.

"I said nobody. Now drop it. You're beginning to make me angry."

"What the hell? I'm making you angry? After everything I've done for you? I work every night for you. I'm risking my life for your ass. And you're upset? You're unbelievable," I said to him, reaching inside my brassiere and pulling out all of the money I made and throwing it at him.

"Here. That's for your ungrateful ass. Not that you care, but I made your money tonight, sir. Would you like for me to suck your dick, too, sir?" I said with an attitude as I walked away. I heard him running after me. He pinned me to the wall and punched me in the face so hard that I fell to the floor, crying.

"Don't you ever in your life talk to me like that? You better learn some damn respect. I'm the one that's taking care of your ass. I'm the one that's providing a roof over your damn head. Who the hell else wants to take you in? Nobody! Nobody else wants you. So you need to be appreciative of all the things you're getting from me. So, if you see me with another bitch up in here, it's not your place to try and break nothing up. You act like you don't see shit. You hear me?"

"What? That doesn't make any sense," I replied fearfully. "I thought I was your girl. I thought that I meant something to you? How can you do this to me?" I began crying silently as he continued to crush my spirit with his abrasive words.

"What? You thought you were my girl? All you are Danielle is an easy ho. I fucked you for money, and now I got you tricking for me. You're not special, Danielle, and you never will be. You work for me. You use that body to get what you want. It's all you're capable of doing."

I sat there on the floor crying my eyes out and holding my face.

The next morning, I was still upset about what took place the night before. I wanted to leave. I really wanted to be able to pack my shit up and go, but what pained me the most was that I knew that I couldn't. Knowing that he had that much control over me brought me to tears all over again. I heard the door open and close, Dante was home. He began calling out to me, but I remained silent. I hated the person he had become. He had tricked me into believing that he genuinely cared for me.

"Danielle, didn't you hear me calling you? What's wrong? Why are you crying?" Dante questioned me as he entered the bedroom.

"I think you know why, Dante. Look at what you've put me through. You've changed. I thought you loved me."

"I do love you, Danielle. That girl didn't mean anything to me. You're here with me. I apologize, Danielle. You know how it is between us, D. I'm the only one taking care of you. If I didn't love you, you wouldn't be here in my house," he said, trying to convince me.

I stared down at the floor, trying to internalize what he was saying. He began kissing my neck and rubbing my back. I tried to brush him off, but he pulled me closer toward him. I rolled my eyes at him to let him know I was simply not in the mood. But he ignored my response while he began undressing me. I knew at that moment that Dante wasn't going to do what I wanted. I gave into him as his body towered over me. I couldn't lie. I did miss sex with Dante. He was amazing, and he knew just how to make me weak. *What am I doing?* Things were becoming blurred. One minute, we were together. Then, the next minute, we were fighting, and now we were making love. Everything inside of me wanted to run away from him, but my body screamed for his tight embrace. I didn't know what love felt like, but I knew I couldn't afford to lose this feeling with Dante.

Later that evening, Dante told me he had someplace to take me. I thought we would be going somewhere special. But we end up at the Coliseum, a damn strip club at 8 Mile and Gratiot. I wondered what was going through his mind to bring me here. Never in my life had I seen such a site. The club was packed with men of all ages, most throwing money at women as they paraded around provocatively on the stage. As we found ourselves a private table somewhere in the back, I looked over to see Dante smiling at me.

"This is where all the money is made! Well, the good money. I promise you, Danielle. You can make thousands here. Way more than what any nine-to-five would pay you."

"By taking off my clothes in front of a bunch of strange men?"

"Hell, you're already sleeping with them for money. What's the difference? At least, this way, you don't have to sleep with them, and you'll probably make twice as much money. Don't look at it for what it is. Look at it as entertaining helpless men. Look. All I'm saying is, you got a baby to take care of, and ain't no job going to pay you nearly as much as dancing will. I'm going to let you go backstage and talk to a few of the dancers. I can get you started tomorrow."

What the hell was I getting myself into? I followed Dante backstage to the dressing room to see what he was talking about. These dancers had to be bold to get out there to perform in front of all these strangers.

"Hello, ladies. This here is Danielle. She's going to be starting here tomorrow. Thought maybe you girls could show her the ropes," he said to six scantily clad dancers, who were practicing moves and preparing their makeup.

"So you going to be dancing here, now?"

"I guess, if it's what Dante wants me to do." I replied.

"If it's what he wants you to do? Girl, what are you talking about? If you ain't trying to do this, then don't. Dante isn't your daddy," a girl named Candy stated.

"I know, but he's been taking care of me lately, and I love him so. I—"

"Girl, Dante don't care about you. The only person Dante cares about is himself. Trust me, sweetie, I should know. I was once right there in your shoes. I used to mess around with Dante. I worked for him thinking he would take care of me, but, after a while, he dropped me. He left me to fend for myself. That's how I got stuck here. I didn't have no other family to take care of me, so stripping became a way for me to provide for myself. I just hope the same thing doesn't happen to you," another female said to me. Finally, I realized this was the same girl that I had seen at Dante's house the night before.

"Wait a minute. Aren't you the same girl that was at his house the other night?"

"Yeah, I thought we had a chance to work things out, but then I saw you there. That's what I'm saying. Don't let Dante control you. Make your own money. That's what I'm trying to do. By the way, my name is Charde, but, on the stage, I'm Chardonnay."

"Well, how much cash do you ladies make a night?" I questioned.

I didn't know how honest Charde was being, but Dante had changed recently, so I didn't know how long my meal ticket would last. Maybe this would be a good way for me to get on my feet finally. For so very long, I'd always depended on other people to take care of me. Perhaps, this would be the start of me finding my independence.

"I usually make between four to six hundred dollars a night. But it depends on what you're doing—dancing on stage or giving a private dance. I will say this. I make in a week what regular working people make in a month," Candy explained to me.

"Damn! Really? I need to get in on this," I said excitedly.

"Well, it's time for us to go back on stage again. I guess we'll be seeing you again, new girl." Candy said to meas she exited the dressing room. I turned to follow the girls to see what they did when Charde called me back in.

"Hey, new girl. Look. I'm not trying to get all up in your business. But I just don't want you making the mistake of thinking a man will take care of you. That's what I thought. Now, I'm twenty-three years old working as a stripper. Don't do that. I thought he loved me, too. He wined and dined me in the beginning, but that shit changed real quickly. Then, I became stuck with nowhere else to go. How old are you?"

"Seventeen," I answered.

"Yeah, I was around that age. I was nineteen years old when I hooked up with Dante. Just watch yourself with Dante. Don't let yourself...don't let yourself get trapped. If you're going to do this, use this money as a way to get as far away from him as possible. I really don't want you to end up like me. You're so innocent. That's it! Your new name is Enosynce. Like they said in *Playa's Club*, 'make the money; don't let it make you,'" she said.

I laughed at her reference to the film and walked back out toward the club. I decided I would take her advice and save the money I made here to get myself together. I didn't know what would transpire between me and Dante, but I did know that I needed a back-up plan. I had finally decided to take control of my life and be my own person. I wanted to find my identity within this world. Who was Danielle Latrice Turner? It was time to find out.

Chapter 15

Enosynce

My first night dancing at the Coliseum was crazy. There was no way I could see how these girls performed every night. I mean, it wasn't that much different, as I was taking off my clothes in front of strangers for money. But it would be me alone with a man having(and sometimes enjoying satisfying) sex in exchange for a few Ben Franklins. It often amazed me, the amount of skills and courage these women possessed. I sat at the bar watching some of the girls dance and twirl around on stage. With any luck, I would pick up some moves before my turn came to get up on stage.

Besides being unprepared to dance, I became nervous as I watched a few guys walking past, staring at me. I got snapped out of my trance once I received a tap on the shoulder by Candy, one of the girls I had met.

"Girl, what are you doing sitting down?"

"I'm just trying to scope out the place. Get a feeling for the place, you know?" I said.

"Girl, you need to be making your money. Its money to be made even when you not on stage. Don't tell me you're afraid or something. I told you. I make hundreds here a night, but you can't be afraid to work."

"I don't know if I'm quite cut out for this. All the men look drunk. They hollering and acting a damn fool."

"Duh, how else are they supposed to act? Why don't you get a few drinks in you to loosen you up? You gotta go make that paper, lady. You'll be surprised how much dough you can walk away with if you stop thinking so damn much," Candy said to me as she sat down a glass of gin.

I swallowed it down quickly, feeling the alcohol burn my throat. I actually took a few shots of tequila and brandy after that. I didn't care what I was drinking, because Candy was right. There was money to be made if I just went after it. I finally got up from the bar and began making my way around the club. I ran into some guys who said they wanted a table dance. I didn't exactly know what the hell that was at the time, and I didn't care because there were three guys at the table, offering to give me forty dollars apiece. I made $120 just for dancing for them. I got over my fear real quick.

It didn't even bother me when I had to take my clothes off and dance on stage. I became someone else on that stage. I wasn't simply Danielle Turner. No, I became Enosynce. She was a woman who had grown up quickly and had learned how to entertain the crowd to make real money. That was what stripping became to me. A way for me to make money. Hell! It was my hustle. I didn't care anymore what anybody had to say about or thought about my life. Stripping and prostitution were my tickets out of the shit hole I had once lived in. No, it wasn't right morally, but my whole life had been one whole freak show, so why should this be any different?

A couple months had passed since I'd started dancing at the club, and I hadn't spoken to Desmond in weeks, nor had I seen my baby Kylie. I missed her, though. But I loved the life I was living more. This life allowed me to obtain shit I that I had never been able to afford before. Dante and I were closer than we had been in the past. He kept me in Chanel, Prada, Gucci, just showing me a life I'd never been accustomed to.

When I got on that stage, the men called out my name and had no problem shelling out their family's cold, hard cash on me, and I had no problem pocketing it as I performed topless for them and did tricks and spins around the pole that drove them crazy. I was becoming one of the highest paid strippers in the club, and I could tell that difference in more ways than one. One day, when I was making my way back to the dressing room after I had finished performing my set, I was approached by Charde, who was putting on mascara. She stopped to talk to me.

"What's up, girl? How you doing?" I questioned.

"I'm doing fine. I just wanted to check on you. Remember I told you I don't want you ending up like me? Well, I'm glad you're getting the hang of things around here. However, I don't want you to think stripping is your way out. You are young. You don't need to get trapped in this lifestyle because, once you do, that's it. Ain't no turning back. Danielle, I know you are probably addicted to the limelight, all of the attention, and the fast money, but I promise you, it ain't all that. It can be dangerous. Just watch out for yourself is all I'm saying."

"Girl, what are you talking about? I love this lifestyle. I make lots of money, I feel free, and I get to entertain and tease men who can't touch me. I can buy myself things I couldn't before."

"I know, and that's always nice, but don't think this is the only way to go. I'm trying to find a way out of this myself," she admitted.

"Oh, I see what this is. You ain't on top of your game anymore. So you don't want anyone making more money than you. Damn! I thought you were a good girlfriend. But it seems to me you're jealous, so you —"

"What? Ain't nobody jealous of you girl. I probably make twice as much as you. All I'm saying is, you can't do this shit forever. I don't care how much bullshit Dante has been feeding you. You need to save your money and get away from this. I told you that before," Charde sadly said.

"I guess, Chardonnay, but I see you're still doing this. So it can't be that bad then, can it?" I replied sarcastically.

"Whatever, Danielle. Do whatever the hell you want to do. Just don't say I didn't warn you when shit begins to get crazy for you," she warned as she walked out of the dressing room.

I rolled my eyes and walked toward my locker to change my clothes to get ready to leave the club. I exited the Coliseum and began walking outside to wait on Dante to arrive that's when a car that looked a lot like Desmond's slowed down, stopped and approached me. I was surprised when I saw him get out of the car. We hadn't seen each other in such a long time.

"So this is what you've been doing lately?" he questioned me angrily as he got up in my face. "You a damn topless dancer now? You'd rather shake your ass at some club than be at home and be a mother to your child?"

"You were the one who kicked me out. You and your mother! Y'all didn't want me there. So don't start bitching about what I do now. You don't know what I went through while I was living at your mamma's house. I had to sell my body just to make rent. So yeah, this is how I make money now. I don't care if you don't like it. I got someone taking care of me."

"You know what? These dudes got your head all screwed up. You need to go home and be a damn mother to your child. You haven't seen your daughter in weeks. It's a damn shame that you'd rather shake your ass at some damn strip club than to be a mother. You need—"

"You need to stop yelling at me. Don't you think I want to see my daughter? But I'm trying to make money!" I yelled at him.

"Whatever, Danielle."

I heard a few guys I usually dance for holler out my name. I didn't know what they wanted because the club was closed, and I was ready to go home.

"So who the hell are they?" Desmond questioned me.

"Don't worry about it, okay?"

"You know what? Fine! Goodbye, Danielle."

"She got work to do with us tonight!" one of the guys said, yelling from their car.

I saw Desmond drive away down the street. I ignored the guys and proceeded to wait outside the club for

Dante to pick me up. It was two in the morning, and I had called it a night, but unfortunately, they didn't see it that way. I heard them call out to me, but, again, I ignored them. I was off the clock. I wasn't giving away any free shows.

"Ah, sexy Enosynce. Come on, girl. Come with us. Come on. You know you want to. Why you walking away?" one of the guys hollered out.

As I continued walking down the street in an attempt to rid myself of danger from the guys , I felt someone run behind me. Suddenly, he wrapped his hand around my mouth. He told me to be quiet and showed me a .9mm pistol. I was dragged to a nearby alley. I kicked and tried to scream as loud as I could. I was brought back mentally to the nights of when my father would molest me. The guys from the club had me pinned down while one of them ripped my clothes off and forced himself inside of me. I couldn't believe this shit. I tried my best to fight them off, but the one laying on top just slapped me across my face and told me that, if I didn't cooperate, he would shoot me in the face.

"Shut up, bitch! I'm taking this sweet-ass pussy. You dancing around the pole everyday, looking all sexy. If you weren't going to give it to us, then we was going to take it."

The first guy from the club pulled out and buttoned his pants up. He then placed my hands behind my head while the second partner forced himself into me. I couldn't believe these dudes were running a damn train on me. I cried my eyes out and prayed for this torture to be over.

"Please stop! Please. Don't do this to me. Please!" I cried out.

"Shut the fuck up! I swear, if you don't shut up, my partner will shoot you dead right now, bitch," the guy said to me as he punched me in the face.

He was rougher than his partner was. I just wanted them to stop. I just wanted them to give me my freedom back. The last guy in their group grabbed me forcefully. He pulled out his penis then pinned me up against the side of a building and began screwing me like the cheap prostitute I was. As he penetrated deep inside me, I felt him breathing in my ear. His hot breath reeked of cheap beer as I felt its warmth against my neck. The only thing I could think of was to pray I wouldn't catch anything from these guys.

Why was my life so full of misery? Things were so fucked up. I heard the faint sound of a police siren, and that was what saved me as the guys fixed themselves up and ran away. I curled myself into a ball and cried continuously. I just couldn't believe this shit had happened to me. I needed a break from all this shit. I hated my life, and I didn't give a damn about living. As I saw it, I didn't have shit to live for anymore.

Chapter 16

Spiraling Out of Control

I tried to pull myself together as I laid there on the concrete, damn near naked. I was in so much pain that I didn't know what to do. *Should I call 911? Should I call Dante, Desmond...what?* Neither of them truly cared about me. I reached for my clothes as I crawled around on the ground like a newborn baby. I was certainly too sore to walk home, and I needed someone to come get me. Suddenly, I spotted Charde coming out of the club. I yelled out to her, praying she'd come to my aid.

"What! Oh, my goodness, Danielle? What happened? Let's call the police. You need to get to the hospital."

"No, just call Dante. He's on his way to get me. I cried.

"I really don't want you going back to him. Wouldn't you rather I just call the police?"

"He's all I have right now. Can you just call him please?"

"Sure, sure...if that's what you want," she said.

I saw her pull out a cell phone, and I prayed Dante would answer. I couldn't believe the mess I was in right now. First, my father raped me. Now these dudes from the club…

"Danielle, please don't do this anymore? Let this be the wakeup call for you to walk away from this lifestyle."

"I don't have shit to live for anymore. I don't care about anything," I cried out to her.

I suddenly heard her talking to Dante, and, as she informed him of what took place, it hit me. He was the reason I was in this mess. Dante was the one who wanted me to be there. All of my life, I'd allowed other people to control me. Charde was right. I had no business being here. But dammit, if the money wasn't so good. I was in a bad situation. If I walked away from all of this, who would take care of me? What would I do for money? Where would I go for a place to stay? Nowhere. I was trapped with no other options but to endure the hell I lived in. Maybe, in some weird twisted way, I deserved to be treated like this. Perhaps, this was my punishment for being raped by my father for all those years. This was the only reason I could find.

Charde hung up her call with Dante and tried to help me to rise to my feet. I struggled as I attempted to find my balance. My body ached all over as I began to take baby steps toward the club where Charde was walking me to get cleaned up. I laid down on the bench and silently cried as I awaited Dante's arrival.

"What happened to you, honey?" she questioned.

"These guys from the club came and ran up behind me. Then, they dragged me to that alley and took turns sraping with me. All my life, somebody has been abusing me. First, my father, then this shit. I don't even know what to do anymore!" I cried out.

"You sure you don't want to get to a hospital? You don't know what those guys may have."

"I don't want to go to a damn hospital."

Suddenly, I saw Dante busting in the door, looking angry and talking loudly.

"What the hell happened? How is Danielle doing?" he questioned Charde.

"She was raped, Dante. You know she doesn't have any business being down here in the first place!" she confronted him.

"What? Who the hell are you talking to like that? You better watch yourself before you find yourself unemployed. Now who was it that did this to you?"

"Three guys from the club. I always dance for them. I think their names are Steve, Paul, and Tyler."

"What? Excuse me?" she questioned, surprised.

"Come on, girl. You had a problem with me ever since I cut you lose. It's been seven months, and you still can't let go of me. Then, you see me with Danielle, and you can't handle it. This is some real fucked up shit you did, Charde. Plotting to have someone raped because you don't like them."

"Dante, I don't know what the hell you are talking about. You really need to get over yourself. It's not about me or you. Danielle is the victim here, and, if you cared anything about her like you say that you do, you wouldn't have an underage girl illegally stripping and prostituting!"

"Why? You did it! And you're quite good if I must say so myself."

"Dante, you can go to hell!" she yelled as she stormed off.

He rolled his eyes and helped me to the car to take me to the hospital. I didn't know if what he had said was true, but I wouldn't doubt it for a minute. I was treated at Harper Hospital. But I was only kept for two days. They ran some tests, cleaned me up, and checked me out, then sent me home. Who the hell needs doctors anyway?

****

Over the next week, I slowly made my full recovery. I was back to doing what I had to do. I had to work; I had to eat. Dante still needed to get paid. If I could get past the sickness from my father. Then, I knew I could certainly get over this.

When I was walking to the living room to see what Dante was doing, I caught him snorting some white stuff that was lying on the table.

"What are you doing?" I questioned him.

"What does it look like I'm doing? I'm getting high off life. Take a hit."

"I don't know what that stuff is."

"It's coke. It'll make you feel good. Come over here and sit down next to me," he demanded me.

"I don't want to!"

"Bitch, I'm not asking you. I'm telling you to sit your ass down, take a fucking a hit with me, and shut the hell up."

I stood there against the wall, shaking my head. He ran over to me and slapped me across my face. Dante pulled my arm and forced me to sit on the couch next to him. Then, he forced me to inhale this white powdery substance. I didn't know what the hell I was doing, but this shit burned my nose, and I felt as if I couldn't breathe.

Dante tried to get me to calm down and told me that the feeling wouldn't last long. He also forced me to take a couple more hits of this stuff. Soon, I was beginning to feel this euphoric sensation flow over me. It was as if I was on cloud nine, and I didn't want to get off. I looked at Dante in a whole different light. Between the two of us, we had snorted all of the coke off of the table. We were high and didn't give a damn. Everything about this drug had me happy. I kicked back and relaxed on the couch, but he had different plans. Dante began kissing and touching all over me. It didn't take long for us to get undressed and start having sex. But something was different, must have been because of the drug. He was so much more pleasurable this time than any time before. Maybe it was because I was on the hit—uh, I mean the drug, too. Hell, I didn't care. All I knew was I woke up to a good morning. This drug had me feeling good, and now Dante was giving me some good dick, too.

Ooh, I need this. I had longed for it so bad. There were a lot of things I had become addicted to in my life—sex, money, men, and now my happy drug. If I could get all this in one man, then I was truly set for life. I figured Dante loved me. Why else would he do all these things for me? I couldn't help but holler out his praises for fucking me so damn good. I had to return the favor. I got down on my knees and began sucking his dick so hard that I knew he would explode in my mouth.

I grew dependent on the drug or maybe it was Dante himself, but somehow he became my addiction. No one ever told me about how this shit would affect my life. So

I didn't care that I was using it. I was becoming hooked. I had to find ways to get the drug when Dante didn't supply it for me.

As the months went by, I found myself prostituting again. This was what I needed to get my cash flow back right. And I knew just where to get it. Late one afternoon, I visited Desmond to see how my daughter was doing. I knocked at his door, hoping he would let me in. I knew things between us were rough, but the child we made together should have been the most important thing in our lives. He finally opened the door with a disgusted look upon his face.

"What the hell are you doing here, Danielle? Shouldn't you be somewhere sliding down a damn pole?" he questioned sarcastically.

"I just want to see our daughter. Why you acting like this? I'm her mother. Let me in. Damn! She's my daughter, too!" I yelled as I pushed past him to get in the house. I marched straight to Kylie's room. As I went to pick her up, she began crying at the top of her lungs.

"Why is she crying? What's wrong with her?" I yelled to Desmond.

"I don't know, Danielle. She was fine before you got here," he said while taking the crying brat from me. Oddly enough, she stopped crying.

"What? Why she cry when I hold her? You turn her against me?"

"She's a baby, Danielle. She doesn't know you, and whose fault is that?" Desmond said sternly.

"Well, fuck it! I'm here now, Desmond. Let me hold her. Let me hold her. Let me hold her!"

"Fine. You watch her while I go take a shower."

He placed Kylie back in her crib and walked away. I began to feel funny all over. I started shaking and felt a nerve flow through me. In an attempt to ignore the feeling, I tried to hold my baby, but my arms went numb. I dropped my daughter on the floor, and she cried at the top of her lungs. Desmond came rushing out of the shower, wrapped in only a towel. He was completely outraged.

"What the hell happened in here, Danielle? Why is Kylie crying on the floor? Did you drop her?" he yelled as he placed her in the crib.

I didn't know what was going on. My body felt so weird. This was new to me. I felt shakes and tremors, and there was no way to control it. I needed a hit, and I needed one bad, but, somehow, my fucking funds were running low.

"What happened to Kylie?"

"She bit me. The damn baby bit me. This damn baby bit me!" I spat out.

"What? She's a six months old. How can she bite you when she barely has any teeth? What the hell is wrong with you, Danielle?" he questioned me.

I sat down on the floor, shaking like crazy. My body felt chilled all over.

"Nothing, I'm fine. I'm fine, Desmond. Damn. Go get back in the shower. I can handle it."

"Naw, I'm going to wait until my mother comes home because something is wrong with you, Danielle."

"No, there's not!" I screamed as I ran into the bathroom with my purse.

I slammed the door and dumped the purse on the floor in search of some coke or some cash, but dammit I couldn't find either one. Fuck! I was going to have to get some money fast. I knew just where to get it. I exited the bathroom then began looking around for wherever I thought some money may be stashed. I saw Desmond still trying to calm down the baby in the room. This was a perfect time for me to walk inside of Aretha's room, so I did, and I searched around for some money. I checked under the bed and in the closet but came up with nothing. Suddenly, I hit the jackpot. I opened her sock drawer and found four hundred dollars in cash. I quickly stuffed two hundred bucks into my bra before I got busted by Aretha walking into the room.

"Just what in the world are you doing in my room, hell, in my house for that matter? I thought I said your trifling ass couldn't step foot up in my house. Now you here trying to steal my damn money. Oh, hell-naw! You done messed up now. Wait until I call the damn police!" Aretha yelled at me, pushing me to the floor. I ran into the living room to escape the brutality.

"You can't get away with this, girl. I want my damn money back."

"Leave me alone!" I yelled as my body began convulsing. I felt like I was having a seizure.

"Danielle, what's wrong with you? Are you high? Shit! Mom, call 911. There's something seriously wrong with Danielle. She's having a seizure or a stroke or something." I vaguely heard Desmond talking to his mother.

I was feeling sick, and I was having a seizure. *Is this what death feels like?* I knew then that I needed to get off this drug before it ended my life. But it felt so good when I had my high. I needed to mentally be taken away from this life I was living.

Chapter 17

Pride and Praise

I woke up to find myself lying in a damn hospital bed with doctors and nurses all staring at me like I was a crazy freak show or something. I looked over and saw Desmond reading a *Sports Illustrated* magazine. *Why was he here? Why was I here?*

"Desmond, where am I? What the hell is going on? I asked suspiciously.

"Danielle, you suffered from a drug overdose. You had a seizure-like attack," he informed me.

"What the hell are you talking about? Why do you have me in here? I don't need to be in here!" I yelled at him.

"Danielle, you need help. You over here stripping, taking drugs. You're not there for our baby. What's going on with you? You're not the same girl I used to know," he said to me as he softly caressed my hand.

"You're right. I've changed. I grew up, and I became a damn woman. Now if you'll excuse me, I have somewhere I need to be, mamma's boy," I replied as I snatched my hand away from his.

What the hell was he thinking, bringing me to a damn hospital? I don't have no drug problem. I need another hit is what I need. I have to find my dealer quick. My only problem is, I have no money. Aretha must've found the cash I stole when I blacked out.

I walked out of that hospital after I'd being discharged and went right back to my usual spot to score me some hits. I knew it wouldn't be long before I found some guy willing to give up his paycheck for me.

When a driver pulled up in a red SUV, I signaled for him to roll down his window.

"Hey, Sexy! You looking for a good time?" I propositioned the first man I saw.

He agreed, so I got in. I began doing this so much that I didn't even find it pleasurable anymore. Only a means to an end. I needed to support myself, and that was it.

"Hey, I never could do this with my wife. She says she doesn't find me attractive anymore. That heifer says I let myself go since we first met. But being with you lets me know that she doesn't love me. You love me, right?"

This old, fat sloppy white guy started spilling all his business to me. I really didn't care as long as he gave me what I asked for. Eventually, this guy passed out on top of me after thirty minutes of sex. Cleary, his wife wasn't too happy in that department either. I searched for his wallet inside his pants pocket and found two fifty dollar bills, as well as a couple twenties and a ten. I grabbed the money out the wallet and got out of the van. I had one hundred and fifty dollars, so I started walking down the street until I saw the dealer standing around, waiting on his usual clientele. Unfortunately, I was becoming one of his regulars. I had been on coke for about a month now, and, when that wasn't enough, I used heroin. It gave me the high I needed, and, right now, I really needed it. I walked over to him and gave him the ten spot he charged for my hookup. I got what I needed, and then I began walking down the street and found an alleyway to hide in to do my drug. I sat and wondered what was becoming of my life. I had gone from a B- average high school student, to a mom, to a stripper, to a prostitute, and now a drugged-out prostitute. My life was getting worse, and I just didn't see the purpose of living anymore. Thanks, Warrington, for screwing me and my life up. I snorted the coke and injected myself with the heroin. I felt alive. I felt that I was somewhere other than here, like I had the good life. I took another walk down the street, hoping to find Dante. I needed to see him, however, I became disorientated. Perhaps it was a side-effect of the drugs. People were staring at me; I could feel it. I could feel their eye balls all over my skin as if beetles were crawling around and underneath my skin. They didn't know me. They didn't know shit about me. I heard voices closing in on me like those people staring at me were all yelling at me. One voice in particular sounded so familiar to me. I could hear someone calling out my name. I turned to see who it was, and I saw Jasmyn and her brother Jonathan crowd around me as I sat on the ground with a drug needle sticking out of my left arm. I was at a low point, and I just wanted to give up my will to live.

"Danielle! Danielle, can you hear me?" Jasmyn questioned me nervously.

"Let's just get her into the truck. She needs help. Damn! She needs help bad," I heard Jonathan say as he helped me rise to my feet.

"Where are you taking me? Get your damn hands off of me! I'm not going no damn where with you! Leave me alone!" I yelled out, turning away from Jonathan.

"She's strung out we've got to help her," he added.

"You don't have to help me do shit. You need to help yourself."

I stood up against the wall of an abandoned building and pulled out a cigarette and a lighter. I had only taken two puffs from my Newport when Jasmyn took it from my mouth and threw it on the ground.

"Damn, girl! Ain't you tired of all these drugs you on? What's going on with you?"

"Nothing. Damn. Why you all up in my business anyway?" I spat out with an attitude.

"Danielle, there's something seriously going on with you. You need to get help, or I believe you'll end up dead out here," Jasmyn replied sincerely.

"So maybe that's the plan..." I answered.

"I'm tired of hearing this. Come on. You need to go with us. You need help, Danielle. You look bad. You've lost so much weight, and your hair and your face look like they haven't been washed in weeks. You look like a damn crack head. You are far too young and beautiful for all of this. Get your ass in the car now!" Jonathan ordered.

"Naw, ain't nobody no crack head, and ain't nobody needing none of your help. I'm fine just as I is." I slurred as I began walking away down the street.

"Do you want to end up dead and never have your daughter know you? If you won't help yourself, at least, do it for Kylie. She needs you," Jasmyn said.

Shit. I stopped in my tracks. I hadn't even thought about her. I hadn't seen my daughter in weeks, and she didn't even know me. Just to make matters worse all of my antics had caused me to lose my rights as the custodial parent. Aretha had petitioned the *Friends of the Court and told them what happened when I locked Kylie in the house.* Freaking bitch. I needed to get my shit together for her, at least. I didn't know what I had to do, but I figured I'd get in the damn car with them, if it would get them to shut the hell up and leave me the hell alone.

"Fine, I'll go."

Jonathan drove to their house and I followed them inside. I sat on the reclining chair by the living room while they both sat on the couch staring at me, interrogating my ass.

"What the hell you looking at?" I questioned.

"I don't even know anymore. The girl I used to know never did drugs. You stopped going to school. What happened to you, Danielle?" Jasmyn asked.

"Hell. Life happened. What the hell do you want me to say?"

"What happened in your life that made you turn to drugs?" Jonathan stepped in.

"Why? Why are you two all in my business? It's not as if you care about me anyway?"

"What? You're my best friend and I do care. I just don't understand what happened in your life for you to end up like this?"

I shook my head in disbelief. I let out a frustrated sigh and confessed to them what was going on in my life.

"Well, if you must know. My daddy use to molest me," I mumbled.

"What? Excuse me? I didn't hear you," Jonathan said.

"I said, 'My father used to molest me. 'You happy now? Damn! I was molested at the age of thirteen for three years until I decided to run away. Nobody did shit about it. Nobody wanted to talk about it. Nobody gave a shit that my father used me as his personal prostitute."

"Oh, my god! I'm so sorry, Danielle. I had no idea. Did you tell your mother?"

"Jasmyn, you're so sweet, but yes I told her. She even walked in on it. She didn't give a damn. She knew he was doing it all along. But she didn't give a damn because it was making him happy, so, in turn, it was making her happy. Nobody has ever cared about me!" I cried out.

"That's not true. Lots of people care about you." Jonathan cut into the conversation.

"Bullshit! Like who? I stayed with my aunt for a while until she put me out. I tried staying with Desmond, but his mother put me out. I take care of myself. Too many people have let me down. I don't give a damn about nothing or anyone."

"How long are you going to keep feeling sorry for yourself? When are you going to get your life together? Okay. People hurt you. I understand that, and I feel bad for you. Trust me; I do. But you can change how your life ends up, Danielle. You don't have to keep playing the victim to your past," Jonathan lectured me.

"What the hell are you talking about? My life is shit. The man who molested me wasn't even really my father. My real father was some John my mother met on the corner while she was whoring. You know, we'd better just get off it and you should just let me be. Damn!"

"I'm not giving up on you, Danielle. Why don't you try coming to church with us this Sunday? You know, try reconnecting with God? He can always turn things around for you in your life." Jasmyn assured me.

"Fuck God! Where the hell was God when my so-called daddy was raping me, making me touch him, and when he was touching on me? Where the hell was God when my mother stepped in and saw him raping me but still didn't do shit? Where the hell was God when I was homeless and didn't have a place to fucking stay in this cold-ass Detroit weather? Where the hell was God when I was selling my ass on the streets for money? Where the hell was God when I was stripping, sniffing coke, and shooting heroine? See, God don't care anything about me, and I don't care anything about him. So don't come talking to me about no damn God!"

"How are you going to stand here and blame God for your problems? You know you ain't so innocent in all of your drama either. You could have gotten help years ago if you truly wanted to, but you didn't want to. You wanted to play the victim. Hell! You probably enjoyed it," Jonathan said to me, pushing up his black wire-rimmed glasses, looking like a damn Malcolm X knock off.

"Let me tell you something, Mr. Jonathan. There's more to life than your little Morehouse degree. Don't you think I wanted to tell someone? Don't you think I wanted to be free from all the pain I've endured? But you see, I couldn't trust anyone from too much fear of what they'd do to me if I told. I was out on my own at sixteen. I didn't have parents that gave a damn about me like you and Jasmyn do. Shit happened to me, and I fucking dealt with it. I would like to see you deal with being raped up your ass for years by a damn family member then have the same family spit on you and tell you that they don't give a damn about what happened in your life. Yeah, let me see you try and handle that Mr. 4.0 GPA, full scholarship to Harvard Law School. Naw, you can't handle that, can you? I didn't think you could. So why don't you try coming down up off your high horse before you fall and crack your face," I gracefully stated. "Now, if you'll excuse me, I'm tired as hell, and I need to freaking pee. Where's the bathroom again, Jasmyn?"

"Um, second door on the left," she said.

"You still need help," Jonathan uttered out.

I left to go to the bathroom and locked the door behind me. After I used the bathroom, I stared at my image in the mirror. They were right, I looked horrible. I hadn't maintained my long black curls in months and I was losing my damn figure because I rarely ate anymore. I spent all my damn money on coke. I did need help. In some weird way, I started to believe what Charde had said when she said that Dante was bad news. But I just knew he was the only one who cared about me. But hell, he was the one who got me started on the ho stroll, which got me started on the drugs. I wanted to change. I wanted a chance at a better life, but that life seemed so far away for me. Maybe I didn't deserve that life. Maybe I didn't deserve to be happy. Everybody didn't deserve to live a blissful and carefree lifestyle. I believed that I was one of those people. God didn't want the best for me somehow. *But why am I any different? What is wrong with me?*

I continued to stare at my reflection in the mirror and cried at the woman I had become. I heard a soft knock on the door.

"Hey, Danielle. Is everything all right? Can I come in?" I heard Jasmyn ask.

I unlocked the door, and she gave me a tight hug. "It's going to be all right. You'll be okay. We're going to get through this, together."

I needed to hear that. I needed to forget about the demons that controlled my life.

Chapter 18

Unexpected Surprise

The next day, I made my way over to Dante's place to get a few things. I decided I was going to stay with Jasmyn for a couple days while Jonathan was in town. Mr. High and Mighty believed that he could "fix my life." I guess taking a few psychology classes and watching Iyanla Vanzant made him a damn expert. But no one could undo the years of damage I'd been through.

When I approached the house, I happened to notice all of my luggage and bags sitting outside on the porch. *What the hell is going on?* The last time this occurred, my aunt was putting me out. I knew Dante wasn't throwing me out of the house. I pulled my keys out of my purse and opened the door. At first, as I entered the house, I didn't see him anywhere. I began to call out to him. But when I opened the bedroom door, I received the biggest shock of my life. There he was, in our bed, screwing another woman. I couldn't believe it. He stopped to look at me once he realized I was standing before him.

"Danielle, what are you doing here?" he asked.

"What the fuck you mean, 'what am I doing here?' I live here. Why is she here? Why the hell are you fucking another chick in our bed?" I questioned.

"Who is this bitch, Dante?" this random girl had the audacity to call me out of my name.

"I don't think you want to be asking about me right now," I answered her.

"Danielle, didn't you see your shit outside on the porch. You don't live here anymore."

"What…why?" I asked, confused.

"Because I I live here now."

This girl just wouldn't shut up. Who the hell gave Dante the right to throw me out of the house, then go ahead and move in some off-brand Nicki Minaj?

"It's just not the same anymore. You aren't here anyhow. So you can be gone now. I'm through with you. I've used you for about as much as I can now. I have to move on. I have to move on to bigger and better things now," he replied, putting his boxers back on.

"I was in the damn hospital from a drug overdose. Dante, my whole life has changed because of your ass, and now you're throwing me out?"

"That's what he said, ain't it? Damn! You want him to spell it out for you or something?"

That was it. I didn't know who this little girl was, but I pulled her ass off the bed and onto the floor. I began socking her square in the face. Dante pulled me off of her and told me to get the hell out and to give him back his key. I didn't know what the hell I'd done to upset Dante to the point that he truly wanted to get rid of me. But what I did know was here I was homeless yet again. Every time I took a step forward, I'd go ten steps back. *What do I do now? Where do I go now?* I couldn't just allow this to ride. Everything that had happened to me since I'd left Desmond for Dante had been Dante's fault. I ran back into the room and gave Dante the hardest slap across the face.

"Everything I've been through has been your fault. I was up in the hospital, and you never once asked how I was. I got raped because of you. I hate your ass!" I cried out.

"You hate me?" he vehemently asked as he shoved me against the wall. "Bitch, I never gave a fuck about you. I used you. I got what the hell I needed from you. Now, I'm done with you. You see I'm on to the next. Danielle, can you just please get the hell out of my crib and don't step foot back up in here again?" he threatened.

"Um, yeah, bye, boo!" the girl said.

"To hell with you. Fuck you, Dante. And trust me, sweetie, he doesn't love you either. He doesn't give a damn about you. Eventually, he'll do you just how he's doing me. You just wait and see," I shot back at her.

"Oh, no, sweetie, I'll never be you."

"Danielle, just get the hell out before I call the damn cops on you. Go, please!" Dante yelled at me while he shoved me out the door.

I turned and walked out of the house grabbing my bags. I felt tears running down the sides of my cheeks. My world was crumbling down. I walked down the street and made my way down to Capitol Park downtown. I found a nearby park bench and sat my bags down. I had to plan my next move. Slowly, I was realizing that my life was heading straight down to hell because of Dante. I had allowed him to pimp me out, take my clothes off, and dance for money. Now, I was strung out on drugs. *Damn. I don't even know who I am anymore.* I pulled out a cigarette and lit it up. I posted up against the wall of a local sandwich shop, and I shivered in the cool breeze. A good-looking dark-skinned brother pulled up in an all-black Monte Carlo.

"Hey, you...what you doing this evening? You want to take a ride with me, sexy?"

"Um yeah, sure."

I grabbed my bags and got in the car. He was well-groomed with a nice shaven beard with a tapered line up. The scent of his Issey Miyake cologne intoxicated my nose. Too bad I would never see him again after tonight. He was actually worth sticking around with.

"What's a pretty girl like you doing on the streets like this?" he questioned me while licking his lips. I noticed him staring me up and down.

"Well, I gotta do what I gotta do. I gotta make my money. Ain't anybody else taking care of me," I replied.

"You do this every night?"

"Ugh, not every single night. Why?"

"How old are you?"

"Damn. What's up with the 21 questions? I thought you wanted to get something going on tonight?" I asked, annoyed.

He was a cutie but—Damn!—he was talking too much. I wanted to see him drop his drawers, so we could get things started, and I could make me some quick Benjie's. I wouldn't have minded him as a regular customer.

"You know what, little lady? We do need to get things going on. But not in the way you think. You're under arrest for illegal prostitution."

"What the hell are you talking about? Illegal? You a damn cop?" I cried out in a panic.

I almost peed my pants once I saw him pull out his
Detroit Police Department badge. I couldn't believe this
crazy shit.

"Yes, I'm a cop, and I've been watching you for weeks
out here on these streets. I'm taking you down to the
precinct for underage illegal prostitution."

*Well, isn't this a trip. I'm being arrested for being under
eighteen and selling my ass for cash.* He drove me to the
precinct and had me locked down in one of those tiny
cold, dark, damp holding cells.

"Do you have anyone you can call to post your bail at
$750.00? What do your parents think about you doing
something like this?"

"My parents don't give a damn about me. Nobody
gives a damn about me. Can I go home now?" I asked,
although I didn't really have a home to go to.

"I'm sure that's not true. Why are you even doing
this? You seem like such a bright and beautiful young
lady. You have a whole future ahead of you. Now this is
going to go on your record. Don't throw your life away
for something like this. This lifestyle could lead to a lot of
bad things like rape, drug addiction, sexually transmitted
diseases, violence, and death."

"Well, it's a little too damn late for that. I've already
been raped, molested, and all that other shit you've

mentioned. Can I make a phone call, so I can get out of here?"

"Yes. But please know there are ways you can get out of this lifestyle. There are always alternatives."

I rolled my eyes as I pretended to listen to his advice of how to fix the crisis that was my life. I picked up the telephone as I was allowed to make a phone call. Who could I call to help me get out this mess? I decided to call Jasmyn's brother Jonathan. He was the only one that actually felt that I needed help. Jasmyn and Jon truly cared for me and my well-being. This woue a difficult call to make, but it had to be done. I dialed the number and waited for his answer.

"Yes, hello, who is this? Who is this calling from a jail precinct?"

"Hey, J, this is Danielle."

"What's going on, Danielle? Why are you in jail?"

"I got arrested for illegal underage prostitution. I need you to come post my bail."

"Why am I not surprised? How much is your bail?" he questioned.

"It's seven hundred and fifty dollars."

"Seven hundred and fifty dollars! Damn! Danielle, how'd you...what the hell were you doing prostituting out in the damn streets? You need some serious help. Things just keep getting worse with you."

"I understand that. Now are you going to post my bail or what? I want to get out of here," I pleaded sadly.

"Yeah, yeah, seven hundred is a lot of money. It's going to take me a while to get that type of cash. Give me a couple days."

"A couple days? I want to get out here now." I screamed.

"Danielle, you are the one who got yourself in there. Now, I said I would help you, but you can't expect me to have that kind of money just lying around. You're going to have sit tight until I get there. But I will get you out of there as soon as I can. Let this be a lesson to you to not be prostituting out on the streets of Detroit. You're better than that."

"All right, Jonathan. Fine. I'll wait. But hurry, please! I really don't want to be here." I cried.

"Time's up," the cop, said forcing me to end my call.

"Hey, look, I have to go. Please come quick."

The cop or Officer Lewis, as his name tag read, led me back to my cell. As he closed and locked it, I felt like a true prisoner. Not like the prisoner I was now. But a prisoner of my life. I began reflecting on my life and the mess it had become. My parents had screwed my life up. My parents were the cause of the madness I lived every day. If I had anyone to blame, it was my mother and that sick sadistic bastard Warrington.

It was beginning to get late, and the lights shut off, so I assumed it was time for me to take my ass to sleep. I couldn't believe that I had to spend a night in jail. But the good thing was, at least, I had somewhere to sleep tonight. I never thought it'd be here, though.

A couple of days later, I heard Officer Lewis say that I was free to go. Apparently, Jonathan had showed up to post my bail. We walked out of that precinct completely on silent mode. I hurried to the car, praying he wouldn't bombard me with a thousand questions of what the hell I was doing out on the streets. Unfortunately, he broke our silence as he drove us home.

"I just wonder about you sometimes. Dammit, Danielle, you're almost eighteen years old. You need to get your life together. You have a daughter that you don't even take care of. Come on. Doesn't that bother you? Do you know what I had to do to get that money? I understand you were given a bad hand, but when the hell are you going to grow up and take some responsibility for your life? You don't have to play a victim forever. God, Danielle, get it together."

"God, Jon. I'm sorry if you feel like I put you through too much. I just don't know how to get it together. It's been such a mess my whole life? I've never had anyone that cared enough to take notice of me before," I said.

"I know, Danielle. I know. You really need to promise me that you will fight to better yourself. I promise that I will try my best to get you some help."

"How about you come to church with me and Jas? I know you don't have much faith right now. But just give it a chance and watch how it may change your life. Perhaps, this was the final straw. Maybe this will wake you up and make things start to change around for you. Danielle, you deserve a better life, and I promise you that God wants to give you that."

He consoled me as we pulled up to the house he shared with Jasmyn. I couldn't help but burst into tears. I'd never had anyone show me this kind of love and empathy. I did want things to change in my life. I wanted to be a part of Kylie life, and maybe even work it out with Desmond. I still wanted to be with him. I hadn't been fair to him. I would do anything to get these hardships out of my life because I truly deserved this.

Chapter 19

Finding my Faith

J onathan finally convinced me to attend church. He claimed it would be good for me. I didn't know about that, but, after everything that had happened in my crazy life, this certainly couldn't hurt. We made our way down to the Second Ebenezer Baptist Church. I felt uncomfortable being in a place of God, knowing the kind of relationship I'd had with him over the years. I had to admit though that this was one big-ass church. I saw way too many old ladies dressed a little too formal for my taste. I even caught a few throwing me nasty looks because I came dressed in my black True Religion jeans, white Chanel blouse, and ballerina flats. What the hell was wrong with that? I was trying to get right with the Lord, not impress their phony asses. I tapped Jasmyn on the shoulder, who was looking down at her bible.

"When does this thing start? You know I don't want to be here. I've never been to a damn church before," I said, irritated.

"Danielle! You can't swear in the house of the Lord, and it will be starting soon. The pastor is about to take the stage. Everything will be fine," she promised.

I rolled my eyes as I saw the pastor finally take the stage. He babbled something about Moses and his people (whoever the hell they were). I was beginning to grow bored until he began speaking the truth that I needed to hear.

"I want to let you know today that everything you have been through is not for nothing. Everything in your life, no matter how bad, doesn't come without purpose. You must learn how to forgive. You must learn that forgiveness and holding on prevents you from growing. You will be blocking yourself from the blessings He has for you in your life. I tell you that you have to let go of that pain, that hurt, that sorrow, whatever it is that has held you captive for so many years. You are holding yourself back from blossoming. I know it may be hard, but I promise you that, once you learn how to forgive and let go, there will be an abundance of joy flowing over you as if you have created a new life. You are lifting those burdens, those heavy demons off of your back. Don't block your blessings because someone else chose to hurt you. Allow yourself to be free. Amen." he preached to the congregation.

"In order for you to become who God wants you to be, who He has called you to be, to bask in the greatness of what you are today and what you will be in the future...don't you know that you need to stop dwelling on the scars of your past?" he asked.

I wasn't one to be shouting and praising Jesus like these so-called Jesus-freaks in here hooting and hollering. But I had to admit, this sermon was deep and hitting close to home. Slowly, tears poured out of my eyes as I started thinking about Warrington and Dante and all of the pain they'd put me through. *I want to move on. Hell, I've tried to move on. But how do I get past being raped and pimped out? These people didn't even care anything about my feelings. So why should I forgive them? They don't deserve forgiveness from me.*

After church ended, Jonathan and Jasmyn introduced me to the pastor whom they decided I should really talk to about getting over the problems in my life.

"Hello, Pastor Williams. Great sermon today. We have a friend here. Here name is Danielle. We really want you to reach out to her," Jasmyn said.

I wasn't up to speaking to any pastor because they knew my relationship with any religious entity was non-existent. But I did owe it to Kylie to become a better mother. My daughter was almost a year old, and she didn't even know me. I sat down with him and had a heartwarming conversation.

"Well, hello, Danielle, your friends say we should talk. What should we talk about? What's going on in your life? Is there something that is holding you back in life?" he questioned me.

"Um, not really. I honestly don't want to be here. I'm not a church person. I've never been to a church before. I'd rather just go. I don't have any faith or belief in Jesus," I replied.

"Well, that is such a sad state of affairs. Why such a lack of faith? The Lord is waiting on you to join Him in His kingdom of bliss. What's the deeper issue that's going on?"

"You're not going to let this go, are you?"

"I just want you to release the burdens off of your chest. So you can be healed in the name of Jesus."

"Okay, fine. If you must know why I don't have belief in Jesus, it is because I was molested. All right? My father molested me at the age of thirteen for three years until I decided to run away. I can't forgive him, not after all the shit he's done to me. Coming into my room, making me have sex with him. I was thirteen years old. I was a child. I should have been a normal teenager. Nobody cared about me. Not my momma, no one. She knew he was raping me. She saw him, but she never did anything. She let him do it. She let him rape me because she never wanted me. She said I was a mistake that ruined her life. No one ever loved me. How come, if God is so powerful and wanted all of these good things for me, he let me get molested? I remember times when he came in on me when I was in the shower. He said he was going to teach me how to be a woman. But he had a woman. He had my momma. He used me up like a cheap whore off the street. Nobody cared enough about me to call the police or CPS. No one considered my feelings."

I sobbed uncontrollably. I was getting all of my pain and agony out today.

"I'm deeply sorry that you had to endure such a traumatic event at such a young age. But, if you must know, everything happens for a reason. Nothing happens by chance. God has a greater purpose for your life, Danielle. You may be called to do greater things."

"What's so good about being your father's prostitute? Speaking of that, I started selling my body, stripping, and doing hard drugs. Plus, I got a daughter. I dropped out of school. Dammit, all I wanted was a normal life just like Jasmyn. She gets to go to prom and graduate. Where does this leave me? I'm gonna be eighteen soon and have nothing to show for it. My life is a mess. I just want to give up. Just take me out of my misery already."

"You have a higher purpose, Danielle. If you didn't have people who cared for you, then you wouldn't be sitting here before me now. Clearly, those two think very highly of you. Danielle, you must learn to forgive others who have wronged you. So you can move on with your life."

"How can I forgive a man who raped me? He raped me? He took away my innocence. He's the reason my life is…this just doesn't make any sense."

"You can forgive for yourself. You can't let go of the pain if you're still holding on to the burdens and letting them weigh you down. Learn to let go, so you can see the blessings that God will put on upon you."

"God don't care anything about me. If He did, I would've never been raped in the first place. I prayed to Him to get my father to stop, but he didn't."

"Everything in life has a purpose. Nothing just simply happens to us. Sometimes, the things that happen to us aren't always exactly for us. Sometimes, we're meant to touch other people by our testimony, and this, Danielle, is yours. You can change your life; you can heal your soul. You can forgive, but not forget. But it's up to you. That's all I'm saying."

Pastor Williams left me with my thoughts and some insight on what I should do about my life. From this point forward, I wanted to take responsibility for my life and finally live a life that I deserved. I didn't know what the hell that meant. What I did know was that it was truly a step in the right direction.

Chapter 20

Patching Things Up

I had been staying with Jasmyn and her brother for a few months now, and, during that time, I witnessed Jas graduating from high school. It saddened me so bad that I couldn't be right there with her because of all the mess I endured growing up. So what I did along with help from Jonathan, of course, was take steps toward achieving my GED. It wasn't as credible as a high school diploma, but it did give me a chance to finish school and go on to college. I attended Wayne County Community College District better known as WCCCD and studied psychology. Hell, I needed somebody to explain to me how crazy I was. As for Jasmyn, she went on to the University of Michigan, Ann Arbor campus and majored in engineering. Who knows? Perhaps I'll be able to join Jas at Ann Arbor someday.

The biggest problem I had now was trying to convince Desmond to let me see Kylie. She was having a birthday soon, and I wanted to be a part of it. I'd missed so much of her life. It was beyond time for me to clean my act up for her. In some weird way, I prayed he would take me back. I loved him still, and I desperately wanted to be a part of a caring family. With our daughter here, I may be able to get something I'd never had before. She deserved a mother, even if I didn't know how to be one. It wasn't her fault.

I showed up at Desmond's door, hoping he would let me in, so we could talk. As soon as he opened the door, I saw the disgusted look upon his face.

"Danielle, what the hell are you doing here?"

"I'm here to see my daughter and maybe work things out with you."

"You got to be kidding me, right? You aren't the type of person I want around my child. First, you bail out on me. Then, you get hooked on drugs, strip at clubs, and do God knows what else. Then you tried to steal money from my mother? You damn near killed my baby. No, I can't go there with you. I'm glad I received full custody," he admitted to me.

"But I've changed, Desmond. I've gotten myself together. I'm clean. I'm not using that mess anymore. Come on, Desmond. I'm her mother," I begged him.

"Just because I busted a nut in you doesn't make you a fit mother. Excuse me, Danielle, but I got to go," he said as he closed the door in my face. I was hurt by what he said, but I had to admit that it was true after everything I'd put him through. I knocked on the door again hoping to get clear to him.

"Desmond, Desmond, please open the door!"

"Dammit, Danielle! What do you want? I told you what I was going to do. I'm actually in the process of moving into my own apartment with me and Kylie now."

"That's great. But please don't take her away from me. I don't want to lose her or you. I love you, Desmond, and this is hard because I've never had anyone love or care about me. I just want you to forgive me, so we can be a family. I miss my daughter."

"How am I supposed to know that you ain't gon' run out on me again? Kylie needs stability in her life. Not someone who—"

"Desmond, who you talking to? Who is that? Danielle, what the hell are you doing here? I know you not trying to get back with my son. I know you not even back in my house after that damn stunt you pulled. I already told him to get full custody of the baby. So you just need to get the hell out of here!" Aretha cut into the conversation.

"Mom, I got this!" he said to her as he closed the door behind himself, and we sat down to talk on the porch.

As he stared at me, I realized how much I missed the good times we had. Damn, he was still fine as hell. I'd missed him so much.

"You know what, Danielle? This is hard for me. You really put me through a lot. I understand you went through a lot growing up. As much as I care about you, I have to think about what's best for our baby. I know you love Kylie, and I will never stop you from being a part of her life, but I must protect her. I'm just not sure about having you around her yet. You can still come visit her."

"I guess I'll just have to live with that, as long as it means I still can be a part of her life."

"Yeah, always. I don't know about us right now. Let's just begin by raising our daughter together."

I can't say that I was completely satisfied with Desmond's decisions, but I was grateful that I could attempt to reconcile things with him. It was tough hearing him say those things to me, but I knew what I had done, and I had to live with that. At the end of the day, I realized the only people I was hurting was my daughter and me. Now this time around, I could finally have a chance at my own family and giving my child the love no one ever showed me.

Chapter 21

My Revenge
A Year Later

I was in the middle of my Poli-Sci (political science) class, when my cell phone started vibrating. My professor was lecturing about some stuff for our next exam, so I tried to ignore the call. But unfortunately, whoever it was wouldn't get the hint. When I checked my phone, I had four missed calls, two voicemail messages and six texts. *Damn, what the hell is going on that is so important, they felt the need to blow up my phone?* I didn't recognize the number, so I was reluctant to answer it.

I tapped my friend Tara on the shoulder and told her to take notes for me and that I'd be right back. I walked out of the classroom and into the hallway. I had a tingle in my gut that this wasn't good news. I dialed the number, and, to my surprise, it was my stuck up ass cousin, Sadie.

"Sadie, what are you calling me for? We never talk on the phone," I said.

"I'm sorry, Danielle, to come at you like this. But your mom has been in a severe car accident. She's...she's on life support fighting for her life, Danielle. She's going to die, the doctors think. Everyone's down here. We've all been trying to reach you to come see her," she confessed sadly.

"You're kidding, right? Oh, well, if she dies, she dies. We're all going to go someday, right?"

"Danielle, this is your mother!" she snapped at me.

"Fine, Sadie. I'll go down there. What hospital is she at?" I gave in.

"Harper Hospital, fourth floor, room 1B. Please come quick!" she ordered before ending the call.

I didn't know what to believe. I didn't know whether to be sad because I may be losing my mother, or relieved that the bitch that never gave a damn about me was finally getting what was coming to her.

I left the campus and caught the shuttle bus down toward Woodward and John R. There were no tears of sympathy coming from me. Not an ounce of sadness poured out of me whatsoever. I explained to the front desk clerk at the hospital that I was going to see my mother. She gave me a badge and pointed me in the direction of the elevators. I stepped off the freight and saw a few familiar faces all crying and consoling one another. I walked into the room and saw my mother all bandaged up with all types of IVs and tubes running through her body.

"Oh, Danielle, you made it. I'm so sorry. Doctors are requesting an answer about your mother. They say she could fall into a persistent vegetative state if we keep her going. I just don't know what we're going to do. This is such a hard decision to make," my aunt Tralene said emotionally.

"What happened to her?"

"She was driving and fell asleep at the wheel and collided with a semi-truck."

"Bullshit! She was high. I know it!"

"Danielle, please this is your mother," Sadie stepped in.

"Well, the paramedics did say she had unknown foreign substances in her system. So she might have been, but, Danielle, this is a woman who has given you life. You need to be respectful to your mother," my aunt continued.

"My mother, my mother? To hell with my mother."

"Danielle, that's no way to speak about your mother!" Aunt Tralene spat out.

"You're right. I should be talking to her. You were never there for me. You never cared about me. So guess what? I don't give a damn about what happens to you.

As a matter of fact, pull the plug, pull the goddamn plug. I don't care if you live or die!" I yelled out.

At this point, I had no sympathy for the woman who gave me life. I didn't give a damn that my family was growing disgusted by me. It was time to expose the truth that I'd kept bottled inside for so very long.

"Danielle, that is enough of your foolish behavior. Have you no respect for the woman who took care of you?" another one of my aunt's said that I rarely ever got to see. "This is your family," she said.

"Family? Family? Fuck the family. Yes, I said it. To hell with this family. What kind of family allows a teenager to get raped and not say shit? I was getting raped and molested by a man I thought was my father for years and not once did anybody put a stop to it. Not once did anybody try and talk to me. Nobody cared enough to question why the fuck my mother would allow her only daughter to go through this torture. I know all of you knew about this. I know it. Nobody ever thought about my feelings and how this shit affected me. Don't come talking to me about no damn family," I cried out.

Now everyone was silent. There were no words said. The room grew silent. I looked around at everyone with utter disbelief that, even to this day, no one could reach out to me.

"Still none of you can say anything to comfort me? Wow, I guess family really doesn't mean shit nowadays, does it?" I mumbled before I left the hospital room.

I began walking down the hallway, and, before I pressed the down button on the elevator, my Aunt Tralene tried to stop me.

"Danielle, Danielle, stop! Wait. Look, I don't know what happened between you and your mother, but I do know that you can't go through life holding on to grudges. You're going to wake up one day wishing you had built a relationship with your mother."

"Really? The same woman who never believed me when I told her Warrington was molesting me? The same woman who witnessed him do this herself, but stood by and did nothing. The same woman who told me straight to my face that I had ruined her life. Yeah, I'll really miss that."

"Danielle, I'm sorry that all of this happened to you. I swear I didn't know. I would've done something a long time ago," my aunt said sincerely.

"Thanks, but I guess it's a little too late for that now, huh?" I said as the elevator doors opened.

While I made my way through the lobby heading for the exit, I received a phone call praying it wasn't Sadie telling me to turn around because clearly that wasn't about to happen. I answered the mysterious phone call, wishing I truly hadn't again. It was the devil himself Warrington calling me. He said he wanted to see how I was holding up since the tragic accident regarding my mother.

I took the number 53 bus to Jefferson and Beaubien to go pay Warrington a visit. This would definitely be a moment worth remembering. Funny, my mother and Warrington not being together anymore. Somehow they had a guilty conscience about the bullshit they had put me through. Plus, my father or whatever the hell he was had tried to kill my mother one night when he came home intoxicated. I guess my mother made him leave. Whatever, those sick fucks deserved one another.

I slowly made my way up to this apartment. The funky smell of urine and animal feces in the hallway almost made my stomach turn. The drunk I tripped over climbing up the stairs was asleep in the corner with a 40 ounce bottle of Schlitz Malt Liquor in his hand. I slowly made my way up to his apartment door 4A which I noticed was halfway open. As I knocked, I felt needles poking me in the stomach. Something didn't feel right, but I proceeded in anyway.

His apartment was small and rundown. It reeked of alcohol and mustiness, along with a faint smell of mari-juana. I could tell he wasn't doing well, and there were dirty dishes piled up in the sink. I even saw a roach crawl out from a hole in the wall. Everything in me screamed for me to get the hell out of there, but I had to see what he wanted. I was now an adult. There wasn't any need to be living in constant fear of him anymore. I called out to him, wishing he'd hurry up, so I could leave.

"Is that you, Danielle? I'm coming. Just give me a minute," he said from the back room.

I could tell he was getting high. The fumes tickled my noise. Suddenly, he came from the room with a dazed look in his eye. His beard was full yet nappy, as if it had been poorly maintained. His eyes were yellow, which stemmed from years of alcoholism. He was still a decent-looking forty-something old ass perverted son of a bitch.

"Hey, Danielle. How you doing? I'm so sorry about what happened to your mama. Are you going to be all right? I mean, whenever you need someone to talk to, I'm here for you."

"Did you have anything to do with my mother's accident? I don't believe that shit story Tralene told me. Tell me the truth," I demanded.

"What's the matter with you? Why so serious?" he questioned me while taking a few puffs of his joint.

"Tell me the truth?" I repeated loudly.

"Well, one night, your mother and I was you know, we was getting high, but then we got into a fight. She went for a drive after that. I don't remember the rest of what happened," he admitted. "Look here, I just wanted to see how you were holding up about things. You know, Danielle, I hadn't realized how nice you look until right now. Why don't you take a seat next to me on the couch? You've grown into such a beautiful woman. Life has certainly treated you well. Come on. Take a seat right next to Daddy. You look so sexy."

"You know what, Warrington? You're right. I know you've been desiring me since I was little. But now I am indeed a grown woman. Why not give you what you been feigning for, for so many years," I said to him.

I figure, he'd been wanting me for so long, why not go all the way? Hell, at least I was legal now.

I sat in front of him and straddled him like a horse.

"That's what I'm talking about. Come to Daddy. Daddy's home, and he is waiting on you," he said, moving his hand up and down my thighs as he slowly caressed my breasts. I planted soft gentle kisses on his neck as he massaged my ass. I could tell he was enjoying this as I felt his dick get hard as shit. I ran my hands down his chest and began to undress him slowly. I whispered softly in his ear.

"I want you inside me, Daddy, please. Daddy, I want you in me. I want to feel it," I softly repeated to him as I guided his fingers to vigorously invade my vagina.

I let out soft moans as I laid my head on his chest. He pulled out his erect penis and motioned for me touch, rub, and suck it. He wanted me so bad, and I could sense his anticipation for me growing with each second. It was time for me to lay it on him and give him what he deserved. I grabbed his face, kissed his lips, and smiled.

"Can you do me a favor, Daddy? Why don't you close your eyes for mama? I got a surprise for you," I said as I stared into his eyes.

"You got a surprise for me?" he questioned as the remnants of alcohol lingered on his breath.

"Yes, I do. I most certainly do. So close those eyes of yours and don't open them until I tell you so," I ordered.

While he sat with his dick erect, his eyes closed like a toddler begging for a candy. I grabbed a knife from the kitchen and began stabbing him in the neck, then the stomach, all the way to the groin.

"Yeah, I got a surprise for you. You sick, sadistic bastard. You seriously thought I was going to fuck you? After all these damn years. You ruined my life. You took away my freedom. I hate you. Die, you sick motherfucker! I hate you, you sick fuck!" I yelled while stabbing him to death.

He tried to holler out to get me to stop, but he was becoming far too weak to struggle. Altogether, I must've stabbed him ten or twenty times. I didn't stop until I saw that bastard lying in a pool of blood. I vowed to myself when I was a child that I would get him back for all the sick and twisted things he'd done to me. And to think, after all these years, he still thought he had the right to fuck me. Yeah, I know that pastor told me about how forgiveness would lead me down to a road of recovery. But I was a long way away from being recovered and hell if this wasn't a good place to start.

MORE TO COME FROM JMPUBLICATIONS
UPCOMING RELEASES

TAMING MR. RIGHT
MIDNIGHT RAIN

Taming Mr. Right

The Prologue

H ello, it's nice to meet you. How are you? My name is Jeffrey Willis, but I sometimes go by the alias Harold Ian Victor. I'll tell you more about that later. I don't need to tell you everything about me. I'm sure you don't care anyway. But I will tell you what you want to know. I am a young man of about twenty-two years of age. I've been told by several women (and a few guys, as a matter of fact) how attractive I am. Women love to buy me nice things and do whatever with me. I don't stop them because what man wouldn't like the luxury of this? But women usually fail with me because they don't focus on the inside. All women see, when they are with me, is this chocolate brown face with deep dark eyes. They see that I drive a nice car and makea nice amount of money. I am an addiction to most. Once I get inside of you, I never leave. You are stuck with me forever. I don't mind at first, but, after a few years, I start to do damage to the body and tear down the morality of your soul and self-esteem. No one wants to live with me, but yet they won't protect themselves from me. Do I feel bad about what I do to people? Hell no! People are responsible for their own actions. We are a part of an ignorant society where carelessness reigns supreme. We play ourselves repeatedly just for an hour or two of satisfaction, and we don't care about the repercussions of our actions. I remember this one saying I heard, "If looks could kill." I laugh at the mere thought because sometimes they just do.

Before I reveal to you everything about me, I must take you back to where all the chaos started and explain to you how I ended up in the place I am now. I'll begin with my life in high school. This is where things began to get crazy. I must tell you my story. I sometimes like to torture those who don't care about the feelings of others. People are so selfish and thoughtless that it makes me sick to my stomach. The total lack and disregard for humanity is sickening.

Chapter 1

My Warning

I am posted by my locker waiting on this English class to start, and I see Melissa Owens, the finest chick in the whole Chadsey School. She walks past me every day. She is perfection everywhere—from her titties, to her ass, and hips, but she is a complete bitch. Melissa is the meanest and most stuck up girl I've ever met. All that beauty must've went to her head because she walks around like she's the shit. I'd like to beat the shit out of her for messing with my little sister Geneva.

"Hey, Geneva, where did you get that shirt from? I really like it."

"Thanks!"

"Yeah, I liked it when it came out last season. Damn. Why are you so poor? I feel so bad for you."

Hell, if it wasn't for your brother, I'd feel sorry for you," she said, laughing as she walked away.

Melissa made her way over to me. I played it cool like I always did. I let the hos come to me like they always did with their stupid asses.

"Hey, Jeff, what's up? You look good today."

"What today? I look good every day. But why you always bagging on my sister? That shit ain't cool, Melissa."

"Okay, I'll stop. But I can't believe you two are related. You're so different."

"What's up with you and me?" I said as I pulled her closer to me by her waist and stared deep into her eyes.

"I don't know. What is up with us? That's your call. What are you doing after school?" Melissa asked me.

"You, if you let me?" I said to her.

I couldn't believe how fast girls ate this shit up. I mean damn. All I asked was what was going on, and the bitch was putty in my hands.

"What time are you free?"

"I'm free whenever you are, Ms. Melissa. Just one thing I have to know—my place or yours?" I whispered in her ear.

"We can do it at my place; I don't live that far away from here."

"All right. Just hit me up after your last class."

"I sure will."

"All right, sweetie, I look forward to it." I said as I gave her a little pat on the behind.

She looked back at me and smiled as she walked away to class. My sister walked right up to me and punched me lightly in the chest.

"What, Geneva?"

"How can you mess around with her after the way she treats me?"

"Stop worrying. I put a stop to all that. You won't have to worry about her messing with you anymore after I'm done with her ass tonight."

"Jeffrey, please tell me you're not going to do what I think you are?"

"What's that?" I laughed.

"You can't!"

"And pass up on that phat ass. I don't think so, little sis! But trust me. She won't be the same after being with me."

"You are a mess! You are talking about...you are going to..."

"Shh! Everybody doesn't need to know. Aren't you late for class, sweetheart?"

"You lucky. I'll see you at home."

"All right. Order something. You can't cook!"

"Shut up!"

I loved my sister. She was the only one that meant something to me. Nobody else mattered to me. I didn't give a fuck about nothing or no one. I was all about me, and I didn't give a fuck. My pops had already scarred me for life, so why should I care about the thoughts and feelings of others. I just hated selfish people who messed with mine.

I finally made my lazy ass over to my English class, but Mr. Pratt was late, so I decided to catch up with a few of my boys who were in the class with me.

"Hey, Jeff man. I heard you were down with Melissa Owens. Man! Do you know about her?"

"What? That she fine as fuck?"

"Naw, man, she out there. She'll do it to just anybody I heard," Bryant, one of my friends, said.

"Shit's probably true man. Look at the body on her. You can't tell me ole' girl ain't been around the block, but she ain't gonna know what to do once she done with me."

"I feel you on that one, man," my friend Scott said.

My teacher finally made it in, talking about how he was running late because he had a flat tire or some shit. I was only half listening because I was thinking about nailing Melissa's fine red bone ass. I couldn't wait to get her alone.

****

Later that day, I met Melissa at her locker. She was talking to a couple of friends. I tapped her on the shoulder, and I guess she was startled because she looked surprised that I was standing in front of her.

"You ready?" I asked her.

"Oh, yeah, I am ready."

"You change your mind or something?"

"No, I just thought you were going to back out," she stated.

"No, I thought you were going to back out. Hello, ma," I said to her friend Jennifer, a short, little, brown skin cutie.

She wanted to be like Melissa so bad. I could tell she wanted me, too. Maybe once I was done with her, I'd bone her friend later.

"All right. I'll talk to you later, Jennifer."

"All right. Call me later, girl!"

Melissa just smiled and turned. She put her arm around my waist and kissed me on the cheek. This girl just didn't know what she was doing to me. I was ready to take her right now. We walked to Melissa's car. Then, she drove us over to her place.

Melissa lived in a nice home in a quiet, little suburban neighborhood. She was a spoiled kid who got whatever the hell she wanted. And right now, she wanted me, and I was about to let her have it.

"So where are your parents at?"

"At work, of course. They don't come home until midnight."

"Mmm, I like the sound of that. Look at y'all...got plasma screens and entertainment systems. I'm gon' have to challenge you on that Xbox!"

"Naw, I'm pretty good at that. I'll kill you in some Madden."

"Whatever. But we know this ain't what we came here for. So why are we stalling?"

"My bedroom is in there," she said, pointing to a closed door.

"Come on."

She didn't waste any time heading to the room. We locked the door just in case. I laid on the bed. Then, she climbed right on top of me.

"Why you want to be with me? It's so many girls in our school."

Because you're easy. Damn! Why do girls always kill shit by talking? Just let me nut and get the fuck on. Shit! I got other things to see and other people to do. Yeah, I meant what I said.

"I like you. You know that. Melissa, you know you're the prettiest girl in that school. Why you even ask a question like that?" I said as I started to gently caress her thighs and her ass.

She leaned into me and began kissing me passionately. She rubbed her hand up and down my chest and suddenly made her way to my dick. This girl was a true freak! I knew then that what everybody was saying about her was true. I couldn't believe how forward she was. The way she grabbed hold of me and told me how she wanted me to do her. I knew it would be on. I thought about asking if this bitch had protection but what the hell. If she doesn't say shit, I won't say shit either. I was ready to pound her ass, so I could go back to my boys and tell them how good it was to be with Melissa Owens. I flipped her over and started feeling in between her legs. Women love that shit, love getting that pussy wet. I took pleasure in hearing the moans coming from her as she grabbed on to my shoulders. I began to undress her and was pleased at what I saw. My hands rubbed against her D-size chest. I was going to lick this girl out. I finished undressing and was ready to lay the pipe down on this broad. I lay her down, looked deep into her eyes and entered her warm, moist pussy. This shit had never felt so good. What felt even better was listening to her moan my name repeatedly. If only she knew what she was about to get from me. Over and over again, I penetrated her and enjoyed every minute of it, making her come numerous times. Afterwards, I released my deathly venom in this trick. She motioned for me to take the subway. I happily obliged. This silly girl just didn't know what I was going to do to her.

Melissa screamed my name over and over again as she grabbed onto me. The way she yelled and kicked as she squirmed all over the bed was the highlight of all of this. Creating a waterfall in between Melissa's legs made me want to enter her again. Apparently, she was surprised that I would do just about everything with her, because I was tearing that ass up. I bust my fourth nut and called it a night. It was getting late anyway. I had been over there for like five, almost six hours. She looked worn out anyway. I kissed her on the cheek and started to put back on my clothes.

"Are you all right, Melissa?"

"Yeah, I just wasn't expecting all of that!"

"Well, now you can tell all of your friends how good my dick is."

"Whatever!"

"Because, best believe, I'm going to tell them how good your pussy was."

"I'll call you, Mel. Don't have wet dreams about me!"

"Shut up! All right, goodbye, Jeff, I'll see you tomorrow."

I walked home from Melissa's house which wasn't too much farther from where I stayed. I felt really good after fucking Melissa. I felt bad for her, but she probably deserved it. I hoped my sister made something to eat because I was starving. We didn't stay with our parents, we are on our own. My father has life in prison for murdering my mother. Yeah, I got a pretty fucked up life. Luckily for Geneva, she has a different father than me. I was glad she was adopted and wasn't a bastard like me. She deserved better than the life that I had. I walked into the house and smelled the faint smell of spaghetti and garlic bread.

"Hey, Geneva, what's up?!"

"What the hell are you doing coming home so damn late?It's eleven thirty."

"I told you. I was with Melissa!"

"What, Jeffrey, don't you ever feel bad about what you do to these girls?"

"No! Why should I feel bad? She wanted to fuck me? Damn, I should've made her suck my dick!"

"J! Come on!"

"Why do you care so much about her? She treats you like shit?"

"But she still doesn't deserve to be given a death sentence."

"Look, what do you want me to do, 'Neva? There is nothing I can do. What do you want me to do, not have sex?"

"Yes!"

"I didn't do this to myself. It happened to me. I'm not going to stop something I enjoy just because of some fucked-up shit. I like sex. I love sex. So leave me alone. I'm hungry. Where is the food at?"

"It's in the microwave, I'm going to bed."

"Goodnight!"

I knew my sister worried about me. But I was seventeen years old, going on eighteen. I was all she had. I had to deal with some horrific shit because my father was out there. How the hell is that my fault? If I could, I'd go to that prison and beat the shit out of his ass. I hope I didn't end up in there with him one day. But right now, I enjoyed pussy, and the feeling I got from having sex and had no plans on stopping anytime soon.

The next day at school, I was standing outside the building waiting on homeroom to begin when Bryant and Scott approached me wondering how my one-night stand went with Melissa.

"I know you uh, put it down on her, right?" Scott asked.

"Man, what you think? She got exhausted after I busted for the fourth time," I said as they all began to burst out with laughter.

"Shh, there she is," I said as Melissa was making her way toward the door with a few of her friends.

"Hey, what's up, Jeffrey?"

"What's up, baby? How are you doing?"

She continued in the building as we stood outside. Melissa and her friends walked over to the cafeteria to grab some breakfast before class started.

"So, girl, come on tell me how it was! I know that Jeffrey is so good-looking!" Jennifer asked, she was more like a follower behind Melissa.

"Wait, did I miss something?" Nadia questioned.

"I had sex with Jeffrey last night!"

"What? Are you serious?"

"Yes, girl! Let me tell you! His penis is so big! He knows exactly what to do with it, too! I mean, we did it over and over again. He went down on me, too, girl! I mean, we did just about everything last night. I am telling y'all, he is good. I got to have him again."

Geneva happened to be walking past and heard Melissa talking about the rendezvous she'd had. She walked up to her, trying to get her attention.

"Uh, Melissa, I need to tell you something."

"What the fuck would you need to tell me, loser?" she said as her friends begin to cackle with laughter.

"Look, I know you don't like me, but I seriously need to tell you something. It's about my brother."

"I already know everything there is to know about your fine-ass brother. Girl, did I tell you that he lasted for almost six hours! I mean, whoooooooooo! I was exhausted!"

"Melissa, I don't mean to be nosey, but did you happen to use a condom with my brother?"

"What? Why? I'm on the pill. He ain't gon' get me pregnant, and damn, why the fuck is you still here all up in my business? Get away from me!"

"You know what? You are a bitch, Melissa, and you deserve what my brother just gave you!"

"What, bitch? Who the hell you calling a bitch? I'll kick your ass!"

"Hey, Melissa, calm down," Nadia tried to calm her down.

"I don't know what the hell her problem is!"

"Hey, I think I should be heading to the library now. I have to print out a paper before I go to class."

"All right, goodbye Jennifer, see you later."

"Don't you think she might have been trying to tell you something about him? And why the hell didn't you use protection. I mean, I know he is finer than no other, but don't you think that he probably sleeps around? A lot of girls like him, Melissa."

"So, that don't mean he sleeps with them. I got tested two months ago, and I'm clean. Please stop worrying about me. Let's get ready for class."

Melissa and Nadia made their way out of the cafeteria, but Geneva still wanted to warn Melissa. She pulled her by the arm and whispered in her ear.

"My brother has…"

"What, what is it that you need to tell me about him so damn bad?"

"Look, all I can say is you might want to watch yourself around him. He isn't who you think he is."

"All I can say is you need to leave me alone. I am with him, and I don't need you trying to persuade me to leave him. Leave me alone. Damn!" she said, as she walked out of the cafeteria.

That was what I was talking about. Some people just didn't have any disregard for anything. Now later on, when she finds out what's really going on, she'll blame her for not warning her. But by then, it'll be too late. Those six hours I spent pleasuring her sweet body it took only six minutes just to destroy her sweet little body.

Midnight Rain

Chapter 1

Wrong Turn

Late, one rainy night, I remember coming back from seeing a film with my brother Jonathan. We decided to take a shortcut down a side street. What we saw would change our lives forever. As we continued down the street, we started to hear swearing and the sounds of someone being punched. I just knew this wasn't about to be pretty. As much as we tried to walk away from it, we just couldn't. It was as if we were just frozen in fear. A man's deep voice dominated over a woman's small, quaint voice.

"So you just weren't going to tell me? You weren't thinking about me at all before this happened?" We overheard a male voice say.

"Paul, I'm married now. We dated two years ago, and, if I recall, you're married as well, aren't you? So why are you harassing me? You're drunk, and you really need to get home," a woman's voice said.

"I know you're not just going to walk away from me, bitch!"

"Paul, what the hell is your problem?"

"I spotted you at the bar, and you couldn't even say anything. All of you women are the damn same. You get a little power, and you think you're God's gift to the fucking universe."

"Whatever, Paul. You're drunk. You need to get the hell out of here. Plus, I have a husband and kids to go home to," she said turning to walk away.

"Come back here. Do you think I'm playing with you? I will kill your ass," the man said as he ran up behind the woman and pulled her toward the ground.

"What the hell is your problem?" the woman cried.

"I'll be damned if I let your ass make it out of here alive. I've worked for that damn company for fifteen years, gave them the best I had to offer. I should've gotten that promotion, but they gave it to a bitch, and they decided to let me go. They let me go! I deserved that promotion. I was passed over for a bitch. All you women are the same. All you do is take, take, and take. Now I'm going to take what belongs to me. Fuck that company. They wanted to pass me over because of her. *'She has more experience than you, Paul. She went to an Ivy League college. Blah-blah.'* I killed that bitch, too. She deserved it. All you women deserve to be murdered and dumped in the bottom of the goddamn river. Let this be a lesson to all you women. You don't deserve shit, except to fucking die!" he said, pulling out a gun from his side and letting the trigger go off.

Once we saw this, we turned and ran for our lives. We didn't want to be a part of what would happen next. But apparently, the guy heard us because the next thing I knew, he was hot on our trails. We thought to take a shortcut down the alley. It was already dark and, if you couldn't tell, this wasn't the best neighborhood to be in, especially at this time of night. No one out but prostitutes, pimps, and crack heads looking for hits. Just when we thought we were in the clear, he jumped right in front of us. We damn near pissed ourselves. Jonathan stood in front of me, just in case the man tried to attack us.

"Where the hell y'all think y'all going?"

"Look man, we don't want any trouble. We are just trying to get home," my brother said.

I could tell he was terrified beyond belief because he's a pretty tall and muscular dude. So, for him to be scared, we knew this wasn't good.

"What did y'all see?"

"Oh, man, we didn't see anything."

"Bullshit, if y'all say anything to the police, I'll blast y'all like I did that bitch! Do you understand me?"

"Yeah, man, we hear you. We hear you loud and clear!" Jonathan answered trembling in fear.

"And just and case you think I'm playing!" he fired one bullet straight into the air. At that moment, we turned and ran the hell away. I think we ran all the way home that night.

The Next Day

I woke up around seven in the morning. I could barely sleep at all that night. All I could think of is that horrible man and that poor, poor woman. I felt so sorry for her and her family. I walked downstairs to see my brother Jonathan preparing breakfast. I just didn't know how he and I would get through this. I just wish I could get over it. What could we do? We were threatened to silence so telling the police was out. But on the other hand, a woman's life was taken at the hands of this jerk. We were stuck between a rock and a hard place. What should we do?

"Thanks, Jonathan," I said grabbing my plate and sitting at the table across from him.

"How did you sleep?" he asked.

"I didn't. I couldn't get that murder out my head. I can't believe...I mean, what can we do? I'm too afraid to go to the police. But we can't just let that woman's murder go unreported."

"I know the way that guy spoke to me, it's a moment I'll never forget. His eyes burned holes in my retinas and pierced right into my soul. I'm not usually scared too easily but once you've seen a 230lb man with a loaded gun pop it off on someone, you have seen it all.

"I think we need to go to the police anyway, Jon. I just can't live with this on my conscience," I stated as I swallowed my blueberry pancakes and shuffled my scrambled eggs around on my plate.

"I mean, it's just not that easy, Rochelle," he said as he turned to stare out the window. "You didn't see the way he looked at me. He said he would kill us if we told anybody, Chelle."

"So, can you honestly sit here and let this go? What if it were me out there? Wouldn't you want someone to tell you if your loved one died? Who are you more afraid of? Him or God? 'Cause he's the one you're going to have to answer to," I said as I got up and left the kitchen.

I just couldn't live with this on my conscience anymore. Something had to be done. Jonathan and I weren't sure if we were going to go to the police as of yet about this, but to ease my own pain, I think it's all right to share with you the uncovering of this tragic tale. So, as you may already know, the woman was an ex-girlfriend of the guy who apparently received a bad hand at his job by being demoted and fired. But since the situation touched so close to home, I will tell you everything that I know.

Chapter 2

It Started One Night

Paul Donaldson was shuffling files on his desk while talking to his wife on the phone.

"Yeah, honey. Today is the day. I just know I'm in a good position for this senior account manager position," Paul said confidently to his wife Elaine over the phone.

"Well, I know you will get it. I wish you the best! Oh, Aiden just woke up."

"Oh, it's all right. I have to go anyway. Kiss the little man for me. All right, love you, too, honey," he said as his boss, Mr. Nicholson, stepped into his office.

"Hey, Paul. Can I see you in my office? I would like to talk to you."

"Sure, boss," he said as he silently congratulated himself.

He knew that job promotion would be his. But as he entered his boss's office, he was in for a huge surprise.

"Who is this? I've never seen you here before. One of your girlfriends?" he joked with his boss.

"That's very funny, but no, she is not my girlfriend, but our new senior account manager. I know you were really banking on that position, so this was a hard decision for us to make."

"Wait, wait, wait a minute. I've never seen her at this firm in my life. How are you going to outsource the damn position? I've been here for fifteen years. I deserve that damn position. And you're going to give it to this bitch! That is an outrage."

"Excuse me, but, sir, you don't know anything about me to be calling me out of my name," the woman said.

"Yes, Paul, I can understand your frustration and disappointment. But I will ask you to refrain from calling Mrs. Lewis out of her name. You should be respectful."

"Why? I have worked for this company for—"

"I understand that, but Mrs. Lewis comes with twenty years' experience, a master's degree from Princeton University, and her sales track record is through the roof. She has closed accounts with over twenty prestigious companies. Let's just be honest here, Paul. You haven't done much for our company in six months. I've just been trying to give you time to straighten things up."

"This is bullshit, and you know it. I've done plenty for this company, but no one sees it because they're all too busy kissing each other's asses. How'd you get this position? What? Did you sleep with the guy?"

"Paul, that is enough. I expected there would be a bit of animosity between you and Mrs. Lewis, but you are just being disrespectful now. I have to ask you to leave."

"You know what? before I do, you know what, Mr. Nicholson? You are a prick, and you, my friend, can go straight to hell."

"You're fired. Get the hell out of here," his boss yelled.

"I surely do apologize, Mrs. Lewis. He in no way reflects, Nicholson, Gold Meyers and Company."

"Seriously, this is kind of juvenile. It's just a job, sir," Mrs. Lewis cuts into the conversation.

"It's just a job? It's just a job. This is how I feed my family, you bitch. You can't believe that this is just some simple job like at McDonald's where, if you don't get a promotion, you won't get that $0.50 raise. You know what. I wouldn't start my car this evening if I were you," he whispered to her.

"Excuse me? Is that a threat?"

"That's a promise, bitch!" He said, walking out of the office.

Later that evening, Mrs. Lewis was walking toward her car in the poorly lit parking structure and heard a few weird sounds. She first tried to ignore it, thinking perhaps it was someone else who was getting into his vehicle. It felt as if someone were running up behind her, but, when she turned around, there wasn't anyone around. The words of Paul Donaldson began to float through her mind but, *He couldn't be that upset over a silly little job promotion could he? No, that was insane. All he should do is work hard, and surely he can find himself in the same position as I am.* Shaking it off, she pulled her car keys out of her purse and got inside her car. As she turned the engine on, she noticed someone in the back seat, and her back door appeared to be damaged as if someone tried to get in. When she tried to take a look, there was Paul behind her with one hand over her mouth and the other with a knife to her throat.

"I told you I'd kill you, bitch! You picked the wrong damn company to try and take over today. I'll be damned if I lose my job, not only to a bitch, but a black bitch at that. My wife is going to be expecting me to walk through that door with great news and what am I going to tell her? 'Oh, no, honey, I didn't get that job because my boss gave it to a nigger bitch.' I don't think so. You women are always taking things that don't belong to you. Now I'm taking what belongs to me!" He said as he took the knife and slit her throat three times. He jumped in the front seat of the car while he pushed the dead body to the passenger seat.

Not wanting to gain any witnesses, Paul drove off from the premises and headed down to the nearest river in Trenton, New Jersey. He opened the trunk and placed a black trash bag over the body. He dragged it down to the riverbank, and, with all his strength, he threw her body into the river. He watched as the body sank down to the bottom of the Delaware River.

About the Author

Janae Marie is an American, writer, journalist and publisher. Born in Michigan, she's earned a Bachelor's degree from Wayne State University in Media Arts and working on another as well. She's also wrote, produced, directed and edited her own film entitled, "My Mother Donna." She is also the publisher of Young Urban Voices Magazine, an online publication for young adults. A few novels are soon to come from Janae, such as, "Midnight Rain," "Leilani's Secret," "Taming Mr. Right" and she's the author of the book, "Flirting with Temptations," her debut release. She now resides in California.

My mission is to entertain and educate the world through experiences we all can relate to.